Last Chance

Sasha Welter

Published by Sasha Welter, 2024.

This is a work of fiction. Similarities to real people, places, or events are entirely coincidental.

LAST CHANCE

First edition. November 22, 2024.

Copyright © 2024 Sasha Welter.

ISBN: 979-8224020423

Written by Sasha Welter.

Also by Sasha Welter

Revenge
Wicked Sisters
Last Chance

Dedication

Aunt Teresa – The orator of the family

Dr. Jon Stanton - My favorite Psychology professor

Dr. Michael Storey - My favorite English/Literature Professor

Chapter 1

• • • •

ZOYA DROVE UP THE WINDING road to her daughter's school. The private Catholic high school sat in the center of 12 acres of land. Zoya arrived at the school an hour before dismissal, joining the line of parents who had clearly beaten her to the pick-up spot. After placing her car number placard on the dashboard, she turned off the engine and stepped out to chat with another mom a few cars ahead. With an hour to kill they might as well pass the time with some casual gossip.

Marlene lowered her window, and smiled broadly. "Come on in and take a load off."

Zoya opened the passenger side door and made herself comfortable. "How are you? As if we didn't text each other all day."

Marlene placed her phone on the charger. "Is it summertime yet? I can't stand Mrs. Jimenez. She is so disorganized and she treats the kids so harshly. If I get another note about Sophie doing something minor and being reprimanded for it, I will go off."

Zoya pulled down the sun visor, as the sun was blinding her. She tapped at her head wrap, adjusting one of her locs. "Listen, there are other parents who are not meshing with Mrs. Jimenez. I say bring the complaints to the principal. Mr. Walker has to do something if he gets enough parents complaining about the same thing."

"We spend too much money at this school to have to deal with unprofessional teachers. Teachers are leaving, they have been understaffed this year, and they have teachers covering classes that have no background in the subject they are teaching. How is an art teacher teaching 10th graders math?" Marlene grabbed her steering wheel as she rocked back and forth in astonishment. "Does that make sense?"

Zoya shook her head, feeling a bit overwhelmed. "No, it doesn't. There is a lot going on in this school and it is not sitting well with me." Zoya looked around the circle seeing Jasmine Wright making her way to the front door. She looked agitated. "Oh-oh!" Zoya nodded in Jasmine's direction.

Marlene turned to look at Jasmine as she entered the building. "Damn, something is about to pop off. The way she stomped into that building. You saw it, right?"

"Girl, yes. She did not look happy. Mrs. Jimenez must have said something about her son, Chance."

"Don't let Chance fool you. He is nice and sweet but he does some bullshit too."

Zoya nodded in agreement. "Well, you know Jasmine is going to put on a good face and protect her son. We have to acknowledge when our kids do shady stuff, not just brush it off."

"She's all performative. Like an angry peacock, just strutting around."

Zoya lurched forward laughing so hard as her locs tumbled over her face. "I can't with you. You are terrible!"

"I am just stating the obvious!"

"An angry peacock!" Zoya rubbed her hands together. She settled back in her seat, looked at Marlene and they both let out a yelp that ended in laughter.

Marlene retrieved her sunglasses from her sun visor clip. She continued to monitor the other cars in the circle. "Did Aalia mention anything happening during recess yesterday?"

"No, what happened?"

"Apparently, Chance and some other kids were in an altercation. Maybe that is why Jasmine is here today."

"An altercation?"

"Yes, Chance and two other boys were having words and some shoving ensued."

"Aalia didn't say a word."

"Sophie mentioned it to me, and I really just brushed it off, but after seeing Mrs. Peacock, I had to wonder if that was what it was about."

"We are not going to start calling her Mrs. Peacock, are we?"

"I think you just agreed to it." Marlene chuckled. "Something is up with Chance. Maybe there is trouble at home. Chance has been acting up all year and Mrs. Jimenez doesn't help the situation."

"You can't blame Chance's behavior on Mrs. Jimenez."

"I can't, but she contributes to it. She has the audacity to report Sophie and other kids for minor infractions, but when Chance does something...radio silence. Like, she gives his behavior a pass. I bet you, nothing was said about the incident yesterday, but if the other kid told his parents, they called Mr. Walker and now Jasmine has to report to the school."

"Oh, I can see that. Remember, they never called you when that girl hit Sophie." Zoya clasped her hands together and rested them in her lap.

"Exactly, but they had the nerve to call me when Sophie was just retrieving her water bottle. Is she supposed to be dehydrated? She asked Mrs. Jimenez if she could go to her locker to get her water bottle. Then, I get a note about Sophie being disruptive in class. Kick rocks, Mrs. Jimenez."

Zoya listened as the assistant principal's voice boomed over the intercom. "Let me get to my car. Talk to you later." Zoya walked back to her car so she could get ready for Aalia. The carpool line started up as the students exited the building. Zoya watched Aalia and Sophie run out of the building.

Aalia opened her door, tossing her backpack behind her to the backseat. "Mom, wait for it. Chance is being suspended for a week. It gets worse. His mom was screaming. Mom, she went off on Mr. Walker. We could hear her from our classrooms. The teachers all ran out to look down the hall. Mr. Acosta went running down the hall because they had to get her contained before dismissal could start."

Zoya started to drive around the circle so they could leave the campus. "What? We saw Jasmine walking into the school mad, but oh my goodness." Zoya looked up at her heads-up display seeing Marlene calling her. "Oooop, here it goes!"

Marlene's voice sang throughout the car "Girl!"

Zoya chimed in. "I heard, you were right!"

Sophie started cackling. "Ya'll, it was a riot. Listen, we were in class minding our business and then all you heard was yelling. Mrs. Jimenez ran to the door, and she opened it, and we got all the tea. Chance's mom was going off on how Chance didn't assault anybody, and Mr. Walker was like, 'We got it on camera!'"

Aalia buckled her seatbelt. "Mr. Walker was not playing with Mrs. Wright. He was like you want to be loud, I can be louder." Everyone started to laugh.

Sophie chimed back in "I know, right? Mrs. Wright sounded unhinged. Mr. Walker was not having it."

Marlene coughed in the background. "Mrs. Peacock got her feathers plucked by Mr. Walker."

The girls spoke in unison "Mrs. Peacock!"

Again, both cars erupted in laughter. Marlene tried to stifle her outburst. "Girls, you did not hear that from us. Don't call her that to your friends. That's just for us."

"Chance is suspended. Marlene, maybe you can find out more information. You are always current with school activities and can get details from someone." Zoya continued to giggle.

"Oh, Zoya, you know I am going to get the scoop. As God is my witness, I will find out what is going on. Got to go to get coffee."

With the call ended, Zoya gave Aalia a quick glance. "You didn't mention the altercation that occurred yesterday."

"I didn't really see it and didn't think much of it. Chance is always bothering someone. I guess he messed with the wrong kid this time."

"Do you know the kid?"

"Only in passing. Remember, Chance is a senior. I don't interact with them that much. I only see him in Mrs. Jimenez' class and at his basketball games."

"True, he is a year ahead of you and Sophie. I can't believe Jasmine would react that way. There has to be more to this."

"She had a complete meltdown."

Zoya pulled into the driveway waiting for the garage door to open. "As much as Jasmine is a flashy person, that type of outburst is a bit much even for her."

Chapter 2

• • • •

JASMINE PUSHED A STRAND of hair behind her ear, unruffled by the commotion she had started. She stood rigid in front of Mr. Walker as she reviewed the footage of her son shoving another student. Her eyes grew narrow as she watched Chance ball up his fist and give the student a solid cuff to the shoulder. "Listen, Chance is not this way. The other boy had to have said something to agitate my son."

Mr. Wright continued to let the video play. "Several witnesses said your son went up to the other student and instigated a fight. The other student didn't even react to Chance. Another student jumped in and pushed your son away from the boy. This is unacceptable behavior, and your outburst didn't give good optics either. You are the adult. You cannot come up in this building reacting the way you did. I have the right mind to have you removed. Not only is your son being suspended, there has been issues with his classes and grades. We have sent notice to you and your husband about his grades. He is failing two classes and if he doesn't have enough credits, he may not graduate on time. In light of this, I may have to have him give up sports. His G.P.A is sinking."

Jasmine almost fell forward. "What? You are going to remove him from the basketball team? He might not graduate on time. It's that teacher of his, Mrs. Jimenez. She can't teach, and her class is a complete mess. I've met with her, and there's no way any of those students can succeed with her in charge."

"That is not true. Mrs. Jimenez is very supportive of her students, and she does a great job at getting her students to grasp complicated concepts."

"That is a damn lie!" Jasmine shot back. "There are several other parents who have complained about Mrs. Jimenez and her teaching style. Even the way she picks on students and goes out of her way to embarrass some of them."

"I can't speak on other parents' concerns, Mrs. Wright."

"That is exactly your response. There is no transparency and no accountability. You will sit here and defend your staff when you know they are wrong and not striving to provide proper education. I need to speak with the governing body of this school. If you won't do your job, I will make sure someone does." Jasmine exited Mr. Walker's office heading straight for Mrs.

Jimenez' classroom. She sauntered down the hall and marched into the classroom. "You are the reason why my son is having so much difficulty. If you would do your damn job, we wouldn't have these problems."

Mrs. Jimenez rose from her seat, putting her hands up to calm Mrs. Wright down. "Mrs. Wright, I am doing my job. I have been working with Chance and he is not turning in his work. He is present in class but not doing the work. What he turns in needs a lot of improvement. I have spoken with some of his other teachers, and they mentioned the same behavior."

"So this is my fault? That's what you are saying?"

"I am not saying that, but we have reached out to you and Mr. Wright so there could be some engagement at home which would then reflect improved learning from Chance. He is a bright young man with so much potential."

Jasmine made her way around several desks to get closer to Mrs. Jimenez. "What you need to do is teach. We are doing what we need to do at home, when Chance gets to school there is so much going on here that makes it impossible for him to learn."

Mrs. Jimenez looked around Jasmine as Mr. Walker and Mr. Acosta ran into the classroom. "Mrs. Wright, honestly, if you don't want to see where your son contributes to his failing then there is nothing I can say or do. Have a good day."

"Who the hell do you think you are talking to? I pay your salary. You need to be fired. Look at this classroom. Who can learn in this train wreck for a class?" Jasmine shoved a desk out of her way before knocking over a chair.

Mr. Walker gestured for Mrs. Wright to leave the classroom.

Jasmine exited the classroom, storming down the hall. "You will hear from my attorney!"

Mr. Walker escorted Mrs. Wright to the door. "You are not allowed on campus for the rest of the month. Prepare to have your husband pick up Chance when his suspension is complete."

Jasmine shot Mr. Walker a death stare before leaving the building. She quickly walked over to the parking lot where Chance was waiting by the car. "I can't believe this. You may not graduate on time. They are saying you are not turning in your work. I have asked you repeatedly how you were doing in school and I ask about your homework. You always say you are doing the work and school is fine. Now this!"

Chance towered above his mom at 6'1. "Mom, I have been turning in my work. Leave it to Mrs. Jimenez and she grades my work low. I am turning in good work and she gives me low grades. She doesn't like me and never has."

"Well, something is not adding up. When we get home show me your work."

Chance got in the truck, lowering his window. "Did you really have to behave that way? That was so embarrassing. From the time Mrs. Jimenez opened the door, I knew that was you screaming."

"I was so pissed off. I am sorry for my behavior but I was livid."

"You call it livid. Everyone else is calling it crazy."

"They can call me crazy. I will not be disrespected and you will not be disrespected either. You will be home for a week, and you're not going to just sit around doing nothing. I want all homework and projects that you are missing to be complete so you can submit them to your teachers when you return to school. I need to see what your G.P.A. is because if you don't graduate on time, there are going to be issues. You are applying to colleges. You can't go to college if you don't graduate high school."

Chapter 3

• • • •

MARLENE WALKED DOWN the hall to go pull out a request for uniforms. She unlocked the door and went into the uniform storage room. She rummaged through crates of gently used uniform items in search of blue sweaters. She walked around a few crates full of boys' slacks and reached for a box just out of her fingers' reach. She looked around for the step ladder as she heard footsteps coming closer. She looked up at the box as she stepped up the ladder. She reached for the box, sliding it closer to the edge of the shelf. Marlene pulled the box down and proceeded to step back down the step ladder. Her foot missed the bottom step, sending her falling back and the box was flung to the floor. She caught herself just short of being sprawled out on the floor. She looked at the box cursing then covering her mouth with her hands.

"No need for foul language." Mr. Walker reached for the box placing it on an empty table. "Are you okay?"

Marlene shook her head, her dimples on full display as she smiled nervously. "Sorry about that, Mr. Walker." Marlene walked over to the table to start rummaging through the box. "So, Mr. Walker, is everything good with Mrs. Wright?"

Mr. Walker shook his head, exasperation flashed across his face. "Lord, that woman!" He looked back out into the hall to make sure none of the students were out there. He quickly shut the door. "She just doesn't want to accept that her son is failing."

"Failing!" Marlene quickly covered her mouth.

"Yeah, he really needs to just buckle down. His mother spends more time complaining about Mrs. Jimenez."

"Well, Mrs. Jimenez has a few complaints from other parents."

"I really can't speak on it. I already said too much to you. I trust you to keep this here in this room. At least for the next few weeks, Mrs. Wright is not allowed on campus. I am so tired of having meetings with her."

"If Chance wasn't acting up, you wouldn't have these meetings. The other kids' parents must have complained about the recess incident?"

"Complain they did. Not all complaints even make it to me. So for them to call me, means it was serious and not handled by the teachers and recess aides. Unfortunately, this is not the first altercation that has concerned Chance. If he can just chill out he can avoid being expelled."

"Oh my goodness, is it that bad?"

"It is that bad. The parents threatened to press charges. No word on if they will. I can tell you if they do, Mrs. Wright is going to be annoying. At no point does she take any accountability for her son's behavior." Mr. Walker grabbed the doorknob. "Again, this stays here." He opened the door and proceeded down the hall.

Marlene pulled out the uniform pieces that she needed, placing them in a bag and left to deliver the clothes to the student to take home. Marlene made her way to Mrs. Jimenez's class to peek through the window and observe the class. She watched the class for a few minutes, then looked at her watch. She needed to get to the carpool line and wait for the kids to be dismissed. She waved at the front office staff as she exited the building. She looked at the cars already lined up and saw Zoya's SUV. She walked over as Zoya was placing her carpool number on the dashboard. She reached for the passenger door.

Zoya moved her purse from the passenger seat so Marlene could sit down. "You were volunteering again?"

"Yes, fetching uniforms for a student. Oh, do you need anything for Aalia?"

"If you see the skorts in a size 12, let me know. Tell me how much I owe the school for them."

Marlene waved the suggestion away. "I have some skorts in that size I will snag two for you." Marlene grabbed her sunglasses from the top of her head. "Listen to this. Chance could be expelled, but the reason why Jasmine was here yesterday was because he is failing."

Zoya shook her water bottle at Marlene. "No! He is a senior."

"Right. Get this, the other parents want to press charges and Mr. Walker is aware of other instances of Chance acting up with other students. Now, what I have heard from Mrs. Garcia who is one of the recess volunteers is that Chance really picks on the one boy Brent, and I think Brent was the boy he messed with at recess."

"Is that another senior?"

"I don't know. I will ask Sophie. I will look at the yearbook too so we can get his last name. I want to know who his parents are."

"I wonder how many complaints have been escalated to Mr. Walker?"

"Enough that Chance could be expelled. Don't tell the girls about this either. We have to see how this plays out. I think Chance finally messed with the wrong kid and the parents are not playing."

"Right. It was only a matter of time."

"You need to volunteer with me. You get so much juicy gossip."

"I know, right? Just have to look at my schedule. I do have all my permissions and crap to volunteer. I may as well help out."

"Mr. Walker said Jasmine is banned from coming on campus for the next few weeks."

"She really showed her ass yesterday."

"Facts on facts. That is how the kids say it right?"

Zoya laughed. "Yes, you used it correctly. How are we to keep up with their slang?"

Marlene blushed as the memory of Mr. Walker catching her use of foul language flashed through her mind. "I took a stumble from the step ladder. I was this close to busting my ass on the ground and Mr. Walker saw all of that. I could have just dug a hole and dropped myself into it."

"Are you serious?"

"Yes. Let me go get those skorts for you. I will be back in time for the kids to be dismissed."

Zoya watched Marlene leave. She looked out her window lost in thought. She lost track of time until she saw kids starting to stream out the school doors. She started the car as she looked for Marlene. She saw Marlene walking out with Sophie and Aalia. Aalia waved the bag of skorts at her mother as she walked up to the car.

Zoya waved at Marlene as the cars started to wind around the circle. "How was school?"

"Same old, same old. Chance was unusually quiet today. He had so many people whispering about his mom's behavior, and word on the street is his mom is not allowed on campus."

Zoya smirked. "If you only knew the half of it."

Aalia wasn't fazed by her mother's comments because she was busy texting Sophie.

Chapter 4

• • • •

JASMINE BIT AT HER bottom lip as she strolled out of the grocery store. She walked over to her car and stood there staring at Mrs. Jimenez. Upon seeing her, her body started to get hot. She was irritated to say the least. She walked in between parked cars, making her way over to Mrs. Jimenez. "Mrs. Jimenez, I need to talk to you."

Mrs. Jimenez felt a chill go down her spine as she heard Mrs. Wright's voice. She swung around quickly then took a few steps back as Ms. Wright invaded her personal space. She flung her hand in front of her. "Hold up and back the hell away from me. If you want to talk, we can do that during my working hours. I am not in teacher mode right now."

Jasmine stared at Mrs. Jimenez blankly. "Whatever! I went through Chance's work and you are grading him incorrectly. Whatever personal problem you have with me or my son is going to vanish and you are going to grade him appropriately."

"The grades your son got, he deserved. The work he handed in was not even worthy of a C."

"I don't agree. You are using your position of authority to drag my son's grades down. How the hell is my son supposed to graduate if you are grading him the way you are?"

"My class is not the only class that he has low grades in. Why are you focusing solely on me? I don't hear any of the other teachers having any interaction with you." Mrs. Jimenez opened her door as Jasmine stiff-armed her way to the door. Jasmine watched the door close. She again reached for the door, shoving Jasmine back. "Step back. Get away from my car!" Mrs. Jimenez jerked the door open and tried to get into her car.

Jasmine blocked Mrs. Jimenez with her body. "I am not done talking to you."

Mrs. Jimenez looked around the parking lot as a grocery store worker was coming in her direction. "Call the cops!" Mrs. Jimenez turned back to Jasmine. "Move!" She rummaged in her purse, pulling out the pepper spray, she sprayed Jasmine then pushed her to the side.

Jasmine stumbled into the road, her hands over her eyes, her nose was burning, her throat was burning. She tried to open her eyes but she was struggling. She took a few blind steps then felt a car bump into her. She fell to her knees, then crashed down hard on her hands. She could hear the car speed off. She sat there as the store attendant threw water in her face. Tears streamed down her face as she felt herself being held up. She walked with the attendant to the curb and sat down.

The store attendant sat with Jasmine as the police showed up. Jasmine stood up to speak with the officer. "Mrs. Jimenez maced me."

"Ma'am, Mrs. Jimenez stopped me on her way out of this parking lot. She told me you were blocking her from getting into her car and she felt threatened. A call was put in saying there was an incident occurring in the parking lot. There are a few people here who said you were the aggressor."

Jasmine looked around the parking lot observing the bystanders milling about but definitely staring at her. Who knows how many people witnessed her interaction with Mrs. Jimenez. She fixed her blouse and straightened her skirt. "Well, she hit me with her car." Jasmine squinted as she looked at the officer's name. "Officer Jack Miller."

"Yes, I need you to turn around and place your hands behind your back."

"For what?"

"You are under arrest for disorderly conduct and assault." Officer Miller placed the handcuffs on Jasmine's wrists and escorted her to the back of his patrol car.

Jasmine looked around at all the people watching her. She lifted her head to the sky, and as she brought her head back down her eyes made contact with Mrs. Jimenez who was standing across the street with another officer.

Chapter 5

• • • •

CHANCE SLURPED HIS spaghetti noodles loudly while watching TV. He watched his father pace back and forth in the sunroom. He could tell his dad was getting annoyed. He grabbed a napkin to wipe his mouth and got up to see what was going on. He stood at the doorway listening to his dad rattle off several questions. Chance waited patiently for the phone call to end, sensing something was very wrong. "Dad?"

Craig stood in front of Chance, placing his hand on the door jamb. "Your mother got in an altercation with Mrs. Jimenez and will be spending the night in jail. She will go before a judge tomorrow."

Chance ran his hand through his hair. He shook his head a bit shocked. "An altercation with Mrs. Jimenez, my teacher?"

"The one and only." Craig stepped through the doorway making his way to the dining room. "I can't believe this. Your mom went to the grocery store to get some last-minute items and instead gets arrested."

"This is going to make my life worse. Mrs. Jimenez already doesn't like me, and now my mom acts even more bizarre than normal." Chance picked up his fork as he sat down to continue eating. "What are you going to do?"

Craig finished the rest of his beer. "Well, I am getting you to school in the morning, and I will find out when your mom is going to appear before the judge. Not much I can do. I need to make sure you are okay. Your mom will be fine. Maybe after this night in jail, she will calm down."

Chance picked up his empty plate, taking it to the sink. "I have to study for a test." Chance walked down the hall towards his room. He studied for an hour but his thoughts kept returning to his mother. He hoped she was okay. He was upset not just at her being in jail but for why she was in jail. Chance got ready for bed. It was going to be an uneasy night for him with his mother not home. Maybe he should have gone with her to the grocery store. He could have intervened. His mother always rushed into situations acting purely on emotion.

After a fitful night, Chance got up and started to get ready for school. He could hear his father talking with one of his coworkers. Chance took a bite of the toast that was waiting for him. He looked at his backpack then grabbed his lunch. "I just need to get dressed and I will be ready."

Craig nodded at Chance as he continued his phone conversation.

Chance got himself together as he grabbed his backpack. He could feel stress building on the back of his neck. Today was going to be a long day. He was still worried about his mom and how Mrs. Jimenez would treat him. He walked over to his dad. "Keep me posted about Mom."

Craig grabbed Chance's shoulder giving him a good shake. "Of course I will. I will text you, but don't get in trouble. You know you are not supposed to have your phone out while in class."

Chance followed his dad out to the driveway and got in the car. The drive to school was silent. Chance dreaded going to school. As the car got closer, his anxiety started to increase.

· · · ·

MRS. JIMENEZ STOOD outside her classroom, waiting for her students. She waved at other students heading to the cafeteria. "Come on guys, let's get to our seats. We have a lot to cover today." She waved her students into the classroom.

Chance quickly made his way to his seat. He put his backpack on the back of his chair, then he tapped Greg's shoulder. "You are going to be at the basketball game tomorrow?"

Greg turned to look at Chance. "Yes, someone has to make sure we win."

"Ha ha. You got jokes."

Chance made it through class with no issues. Mrs. Jimenez left him alone and made no mention of the altercation with his mother. Class was coming to an end, and Mrs. Jimenez asked Chance to stay behind. Chance rolled his eyes as he got up, grabbing his backpack.

Mrs. Jimenez pointed at the door where Mr. Smith, the basketball coach was standing. "Chance, you have a few assignments that need to be turned in. I need you to turn them in tomorrow."

Chance let out an exaggerated sigh. "I will get it to you." He turned to exit the room. "Hey Coach, what's up?"

Mr. Smith crossed his arms over his chest. "Listen, Chance, you can't participate in the game tomorrow. Your grades have dropped and until you bring your grades up, you are off the team. You should use your free time to get your class work turned in to all of your teachers."

Chance looked at Mr. Smith, his face flushed with anger and some embarrassment. "Mr. Smith, you can't do this."

Mr. Smith stepped out into the hall. "I am sorry but it has to be done. You need to focus on your schoolwork. This is your senior year, and you may not even graduate if you fail so many classes. I know you can pull this together and return to the team."

Chance watched Mr. Smith leave. He turned to face Mrs. Jimenez. "This is your fault. I submitted my work and you gave me poor grades."

Mrs. Jimenez shook her head, her eyes started to water. "Chance, I expect better from you and what you have been turning in is just not work worthy of you. You are not giving me your best work. If you need help we are all here to help you with your classes."

Chance turned to leave, tears streaming down his face. He walked down the hall then turned to see Mrs. Carter, the counselor. He knocked on her door then turned to leave.

"Hi, Chance, come on in." Mrs. Carter looked at Chance and grew concerned. "What is wrong?"

Chance walked into Mrs. Carter's office, dropping his backpack on the floor. "I don't feel comfortable with Mrs. Jimenez. She's making things complicated. She is behaving very inappropriately."

Mrs. Carter handed Chance some tissues. "What has she done?"

"She treats me differently and she kept me back after class and offered to help me, but I feel like she wants something else from me."

Mrs. Carter closed the door and walked over to her desk. "Chance, why do you think she is treating you differently?"

"Mrs. Carter, she has kept me back after everyone leaves a few times now, and she has been extra nice to me. Then she goes out of her way to harass me."

"She's harassing you, how?"

Chance's shoulders heaved up and down as he started crying harder. "She is just being inappropriate. I don't feel comfortable in her class, and I don't understand why she is always trying to be alone with me."

"This is a serious claim you are making. Are you sure?"

"I got to go. It was a mistake to come here." Chance grabbed his backpack and started to leave. He brushed Mrs. Carter off as she tried to make him stay. He wiped his face with the back of his hand as he went to the cafeteria. That would be enough time for Mrs. Carters wheels to start turning. If Mrs. Jimenez was going to ruin his life, he had no choice but to return the favor.

Chapter 6

• • • •

CHANCE SAT ACROSS FROM his mother. She was released on a bail bond and hypersensitive to everything. Being in jail really disturbed her but pissed her off too. Chance took his mother's latte and took a sip. It was too sweet for his liking. "Mom, are you all right?"

Jasmine took back her latte. She leaned back in her chair stiffly. "I am fine. Don't you worry about me. I am a force to be reckoned with." Her quick smile told the real story. "So tell me about school."

Chance's legs started to bounce as he crossed his arms. "I got kicked off the team because of my grades."

Jasmine's nostrils flared as she tried to hold back her immediate response. "That damn Mrs. Jimenez. I will talk to your coach."

"No need to. Dad called him and no more basketball. I need to get my grades up, but Mrs. Jimenez is not budging on the grades she has given me. I also have late work to submit to her. I will turn it all in tomorrow."

"I can't stand that woman. So no game tonight?"

"I still want to go to the game and support my friends."

"Well, I am not allowed on campus so your dad will have to take you." Jasmine finished her latte and got up to toss the cup.

Chance went to his room to find his hoodie and jacket. He gathered some art supplies and packed his new backpack. He quickly got dressed and ran back to the living room. "Dad, you ready?"

Craig ruffled Chance's hair. "Of course." He looked at Jasmine, his eyes softening. "You will be all right?"

Jasmine nodded before going to sit on the couch and watch TV. "Have fun. If you see Mrs. Jimenez give her a middle finger for me."

Craig laughed as he escorted Chance to the garage. They drove out of the neighborhood and basically around the corner. The school was only ten minutes away. Chance was extremely excited about going to the game and couldn't wait to see his friends. As soon as the car was parked, Chance opened the door waving at some of his friends. Chance waited for his dad and went into the auditorium to find their seats. His team was ahead by five points when halftime arrived. Chance excused himself to go to the bathroom. He ran into his friend George, and they talked about the game. Chance saw Mrs. Jimenez standing with Mr. Acosta and nodded his head. "Hey, I will be right back." He waved at George and exited the auditorium. His backpack full of his supplies, he unzipped the backpack and pulled out his jacket. He walked past the cornfield that was on campus and the lights of the auditorium faded to black. He walked down the winding road to the teacher's parking lot, raised the hood of his jacket over his head and quickly found his target. Mrs. Jimenez' shiny black Volvo was parked in an end space. He dropped his backpack on the road next to her car and pulled out his spray cans and proceeded to spray paint her car. Two empty spray cans later, he was done with his masterpiece. He put the spray cans back in his bag, zipped up his backpack and ran back down the road into the darkness. Halfway back to the auditorium, he took off his jacket and put it back in his backpack. He confidently walked back into the parking lot around the auditorium and found George.

George ran up to Chance. "Dude, your dad was looking for you. He got us popcorn and pizza. Come on."

Chance followed George back to their seats so he could enjoy the second half of the game and some concession snacks.

Chapter 7

• • • •

ZOYA STOOD NEXT TO Marlene and a few other parents staring at the car. Zoya turned to Marlene. "When did this happen?"

"I don't know."

"Whose car is this?"

"I don't know." Marlene grabbed Zoya's arm pulling her back to the car. They walked back to Marlene's car and sat in silence.

Zoya fixed her collar, then handed Marlene her sunglasses. "So a teacher's car gets vandalized and we are just here like whomp, whomp. Someone has to know who that car belongs to."

"That is embarrassing. I mean that seems personal. Who writes 'slut' and 'cheater' on a car?"

"Oh, an angry spouse or significant other. That is some real petty revenge."

Marlene pointed at the door. "Isn't that Mrs. Jimenez?"

"Sure is." Zoya and Marlene's gazes followed Mrs. Jimenez as she hurried to the parking lot and the disgraced Volvo.

"Oh shit, that's her car!" Marlene pushed Zoya forward so she could continue to get a good look. Mrs. Jimenez got in her car and bolted from the parking lot.

"What in the hot hell is going on here? School is not done yet." Zoya leaned back in the car seat. She looked at her phone checking her email. "Girl, the school sent an email out. 'Dear Parents, an incident has been reported to the school regarding one of our teachers. We apologize for the inconvenience, but as this teacher is being placed on administrative leave, coverage for their class has already begun and this transition although quick, will be a smooth one. Thank you for your support. With love and grace, Holy Trinity High School.'"

"Was she put on administrative leave?"

Zoya put her phone down on her lap. "We don't know. You know they are not going to name names. Maybe they will update the parents who have kids in that teacher's class."

"Girl, we need to get the details. I guarantee you the girls will know what is up."

"We don't even know which grade the teacher handles."
"Shhh, we are on the case."
"What case?"
"The case of the teacher placed on administrative leave."
"Oh my goodness, you are so crazy."
"We know Mrs. Jimenez had her car and reputation on display, then we see her leaving the school and school is not over, and now we know that a teacher was put on administrative leave. Something is going on and we can figure everything out. The school pick up line is lit! That's how they say it, right?"

Zoya laughed uncontrollably "Yes, that is how they say it."

Marlene squealed, she was giddy with anticipation. "Okay, the kids are about to be dismissed. Get in your car and put me on speaker."

Zoya happily got out of the car and sprinted two cars down to her car. She turned her car on and waited for the call. As soon as her phone rang Marlene's voice came booming throughout the car. The kids started to run out of the front doors. "Here they come!"

Aalia ran to the car hopping in full of excitement. "Mom, Mrs. Jimenez had to leave, and we have Mr. Jacob covering her classes for the next few weeks."

Marlene giggled with joy. "Do you all know why Mrs. Jimenez will be gone for so long?"

"No!" Aalia and Sophie both screamed.

Zoya started to drive around the circle. "Okay, so did you all see Mrs. Jimenez' car?"

Aalia looked at her mom quizzically. "No, what happened to her car?"

"Someone vandalized her car." Zoya offered no further information.

"What?" Aalia grabbed her bento box and started finishing her snack. "What did they do to the car?"

Marlene jumped into the gossip. "They wrote 'cheater' and 'slut' on the car and spray painted the whole car. It was bad."

Zoya's fingers thumped on the steering wheel as she watched cars drive past. "I hate this light. Anywho, back on track. Were you all there when she left? How did her leaving go down?"

Sophie clapped her hands enthusiastically. "We weren't there but one of our friends was in her class after lunch and said that Mr. Walker came with Mrs. Carter to get Mrs. Jimenez. So Mrs. Jimenez left after lunch."

"But we just saw her leave right before you all were dismissed. Dang, they must have been meeting with her that whole time."

"Oh this is getting too good, ya'll. We need all the tea. It's a fricking tea party over here" Marlene interjected. "I wonder what happened?"

Zoya honked at Marlene as they drove past them. "I am signed up to be at recess tomorrow."

"Yes! Me too. We are going to solve this case, girl." Marlene and Sophie started laughing then said their goodbyes.

Zoya looked at Aalia with a twinkle in her eye. "Up for some reconnaissance tomorrow?"

"Why are you and Marlene like this? Of course I am up for it. Sophie too. Duh!"

Chapter 8

• • • •

AALIA PULLED HER WAIST length hair into a ponytail as she walked into the cafeteria. Sophie held Aalia's lunch as they walked over to an empty table. Aalia grabbed her bag lunch from Sophie as they giggled over their mothers' behavior. "Our moms are a trip."

"Seriously, they are hilarious."

Aalia took a big bite of her sandwich as she watched Chance start to harass Brent. "So any update on Mrs. Jimenez?"

Sophie shook her head, her braided hair swinging past her chin. "We should ask Mr. Walker when we get to class. Really, I think it is just a lot of gossip going on, but I stumbled across two teachers talking about inappropriate relationships with a student. I was coming out of the bathroom, and they had kind of walked past. So the teachers know what is going on, but they aren't saying anything to the parents or us."

"Inappropriate relationship...with who?"

"What type of relationship?"

Aalia watched one of the lunch aides reprimand Chance. Chance was so busy tormenting Brent, he hadn't even touched his lunch. Aalia watched Brent's friends come to his defense, but the look on Brent's face was speaking volumes. He was tired of this, he was bending to the point of breaking. Aalia finished her lunch. She waited for Sophie to take her last sip of her juice. They got up to throw away their trash and walked down the hallway for recess. The girls spent the whole recess cloistered in a corner, people watching. They eavesdropped on the parents who were volunteering. There stood their mothers huddled together with two dads. One of the dads had his eye on Chance. Aalia motioned for her mother to come closer to them. "Whose dad is that?"

Zoya looked at both dads. "Which one?"

Aalia, like anyone with a Caribbean parent, pointed with her lips. "The one who keeps looking at Chance."

"Oh, him. That is Brent McGregor."

"Ooooooh, snap! That's Brent's dad." Aalia waved Marlene and Sophie over. "Chance keeps bothering Brent. So I guess the dad is here to put eyes on him."

Marlene let out an ooop! She stared the dad's down. "Now the playground is making sense. You noticed he was only watching Chance too. Umm hmm. It's starting to make sense."

Zoya looked at her watch as it was time for the kids to head back into the building. "You guys have a good time. We will be here for another 30 minutes then see you in the pickup line." Zoya and Marlene waved at the girls as they waited for the next group of kids to come out for recess.

Aalia and Sophie got to Mr. Walker's class first. They sat down waiting for their classmates to come in. Aalia watched Mr. Walker write the plan of events for the day. "Mr. Walker, what is going on with Mrs. Jimenez?"

Mr. Walker turned to look at Aalia. "She will be on leave indefinitely. An investigation has to be done."

"An investigation for what?" Sophie asked innocently.

"Ah, I can't discuss something I don't know full details about. That is why an investigation has to be done." Mr. Walker waved the kids into the classroom. "Come on in, don't be shy." Mr. Walker made his way to the door to close it. "Now I know you all are wondering why I am here instead of Mrs. Jimenez. Like I was telling Aalia and Sophie, Mrs. Jimenez will be out indefinitely while there is an investigation going on. Now, what is the investigation about? I don't fully know but a complaint was filed and it is best for Mrs. Jimenez to not be here while the investigation is being conducted."

· · · ·

ALREADY LATE FOR CLASS, Chance left the assistant principal's office, only to realize that the class he was running late for was being covered by Mr. Walker, the principal. As he hurried down the hall, he stopped for a quick drink at the water fountain. He was already late-what difference would a few more minutes make? He gulped down a few mouthfuls then spun around, running face first into Mr. McGregor's chest. Chance stepped back. "Excuse me!"

Mr. McGregor smiled triumphantly. "You are Chance, right?"

"Yes."

"Brent is my son. You are going to leave my boy alone. I got my eye on you, and I will make your life miserable."

Chance secured his backpack on his shoulder. "Are you threatening me?"

"You keep harassing my son, so I am telling you, you are going to stop. My son is my problem and that makes you my problem. I am all about solving problems."

Chance backed up slowly, knowing he was outmatched.

Mr. McGregor took a step towards Chance. "I don't think you want Mr. Walker to know about your little art show...I guess I am threatening you."

Chance watched Mr. McGregor walk off. As soon as he was out of sight, he ran to his class. He opened the door, watching all eyes dart in his direction. "Sorry I am late, Mr. Walker."

"You get lost in the hallway, Chance?" Mr. Walker laughed as he pointed to Chance's seat. "Are you alright?"

Chance shook his head as he took his seat. "Now that I am here, I guess class can start."

Chapter 9

• • • •

CHANCE ROLLED UP HIS sleeves before closing the car door. He quickly reversed out of the driveway and drove out to the main road. His mom sent him on an errand. Ever since he got his learners' permit, he was sent out on short distance trips to get something for his mother. Today she wanted a milkshake and fresh fries to dip in the milkshake. As he pulled into a parking spot he could see some of his classmates hanging out. He quickly got out of the car and made his way over to them. "What are you all doing all the way over here?"

Josiah waved at Chance. "Our moms are inside ordering food."

Chance fist bumped Josiah and Eric, then took a seat next to them. "I am here to get my mom fries and a milkshake."

Josiah pointed at the car. "Nice car. Your dad got the new BMW. That's hot!"

Chance pointed at the car. "He didn't get rid of his other BMW. I think he is going to give me his old one."

"That would be so dope. I need my parents to give me a car. My dad doesn't trust me with a car because he thinks I will drive fast and hard." Eric waved the thought away.

"You do drive hard, though." Chance laughed as he gave Eric's foot a quick kick.

"Bro, really?"

Josiah handed Chance a piece of gum. "What is going on with Mrs. Jimenez?"

Chance opened the container of gum, tossing a piece in his mouth. "She has been acting up for a while now. She keeps flirting with folks. You haven't seen it?"

Josiah nodded a bit skeptical. "I guess. I never saw it that way but maybe she was. Do you know which student made the complaint?"

Chance chewed on the gum as he thought about his response. "No, but I have been telling you all that she is not right."

"You have been telling us. I guess we weren't paying attention. The truth will come out."

Josiah turned to look at his mom exit the restaurant. "My mom has been asking questions ever since the letter was sent to the parents. The letter didn't mention Mrs. Jimenez but she is the only teacher who is gone."

"If you see something, you need to say something. We got to help our classmates out. You know predators come in all forms."

"True. My parents had a whole conversation with me after the letter." Josiah and Eric got up to follow their moms to their cars. "See you at school."

Chance got up and ran into the restaurant to put in his mom's order and get back to the house. He quickly got in the line waiting for his turn. He put his hands in his pockets then he heard an exasperated gasp behind him. He turned and looked Mrs. Jimenez up and down. "Hi, Mrs. Jimenez. How's life?"

Mrs. Jimenez crossed her arms over her chest. "Chance, I can't catch a break from your family. First your mom and now you."

"Yeah, that wasn't cool. You got my mom arrested."

Mrs. Jimenez shot Chance a look of disgust. "Your mother was in my face acting like a nut. I had every right to get the police involved. I understand that you want to defend your mother, very noble of you, but you have to understand she really came at me crazy and I felt threatened. Listen, I shouldn't even be talking to you so I will take my leave."

"Hey, Mrs. Jimenez, have a nice day." Chance stepped forward to place his order then walked over to the back wall, staring out the window at Mrs. Jimenez as she sat in her car. It looked like she got most of the graffiti removed from her car. He watched her having a very animated conversation with the guy in the car, maybe that was her husband. Chance looked at his phone seeing his mom's smiling face flash on the screen. "Your order is almost done, Mom."

Jasmine let out a staggered sigh. "We need to talk when you get home. The school called and relayed the conversation you had with Mrs. Carter. You said nothing to us, and I have to hear about this from the school. I just about cursed Mr. Walker out because we have complained about that teacher all year and now this."

"Mom, all I told Mrs. Carter is that I don't feel comfortable around Mrs. Jimenez. She comes at me funny."

"We need to get an understanding of what she does to make you uncomfortable. The way Mr. Walker was talking it was as if she has been inappropriate with you and my brain is heading straight to immoral liberties. Has she touched you? I will sue the bricks out of that school."

Chance grabbed the bag and milkshake while using his other hand to hold the phone. "Mom, she hasn't touched me, but she does make me feel uncomfortable. She behaves inappropriately with some classmates, but they may not even realize that it's not appropriate behavior."

"Oh, really?" Jasmine lowered her voice as she could feel anger starting to build up in her. "Come on home. Your father and I need to get our ducks in a row before I respond to the school."

Chance exited the restaurant. He made sure to make direct eye contact with Mrs. Jimenez giving her a nod as he got into the car. He started laughing to himself as he drove off. It was about to get interesting.

Chapter 10

• • • •

AALIA PULLED HER HAIR into a high ponytail. She ran down the stairs to join Sophie and Marlene. Marlene and Zoya sat in the living room gossiping while eating. Sophie shoveled food into her mouth. "Hungry much?"

Sophie chewed quickly then swallowed. "Listen, I don't play with your mom's cooking. This curry chicken is bomb!" She continued eating.

"You are tearing that food up!" Aalia started to eat her food as she looked into the living room. "They are doing a lot of laughing over there."

"Girl, something is going down. So what I heard is my mom got a text message from another parent and word on the street is Mrs. Jimenez was trying to mess with one of her students."

"No!" Aalia dropped her fork onto her plate, the clanking noise drawing the attention of her mom. "I'm good over here."

"So the investigation Mr. Walker wasn't trying to give details on is about her having an inappropriate relationship with a student. No word on who the student is, but there may be other students who come forward with details."

"That is not Mrs. Jimenez. She wouldn't do that."

"We don't know her!"

"Oh my goodness, don't do her like that."

"I'm just saying, we don't really know her like that. She can be a bit much with some students, and now that I think about it, it's usually the male students."

"You are doing too much. Her life could be ruined off of lies. This is a serious accusation."

Sophie got up to get another plate of food. This time, she grabbed a roti skin and spooned out some chicken and potatoes. "What are these beans called?"

"Chickpeas and we call the curried chickpeas channa." Zoya smiled at Sophie. "You always put a hurt on my cooking."

Sophie smiled back at Zoya. "Yuh done know! Did I say it right?" She looked at Zoya then Aalia before heading back to the table.

"You need to work on the accent but yes, you said it right." Zoya grabbed the wine bottle as she went back to join Marlene.

Sophie shoved the curry drenched roti into her mouth. "This is so good. Hope your dad gets in before I finish everything. He's about to be hungry."

Aalia kicked Sophie's leg playfully. "Please leave some food for my dad. He needs nourishment after saving lives at the hospital."

Sophie licked her fingers free of the curry and bits of roti. "It's a good thing I am full because I was about to get me a third plate." Sophie wiped her hands with her napkin then took a big gulp of her soda.

Aalia looked past Sophie at her mother. There was no way Mrs. Jimenez was guilty of what she was being accused of. She used her fork to stab at the curried chicken on her plate. "I don't know. I just don't see Mrs. Jimenez like that. We can't dismiss what the accuser is saying. We just don't know."

Sophie rested her chin on the heel of her palm. "We may never find out who the accuser is."

"But we can try and defend Mrs. Jimenez."

"How do we do that?"

"I don't know, but if we get questioned, that is our time to speak up."

"You are assuming they will talk to us."

Marlene walked over to the dining room table to retrieve the bottle of wine. "What are you girls getting into?"

Sophie inched her now empty glass toward her mom then watched as she poured some wine into her glass. "We are wondering if we can speak on Mrs. Jimenez' behalf. Aalia doesn't think she did what they are saying she did."

"That is very nice of you but the investigation really has to center around what the complainant is alleging. Not that I know the process. I am just spit balling over here. I don't even see where you two would be in the investigation. We don't even know who the complainant is. We can try and guess but that seems difficult. So many variables." Marlene started to mull over various thoughts in her head. She pointed the bottle of wine at Aalia. "You want some wine? Can Aalia have wine?"

"Aalia doesn't like wine. Now she will drink a beer. Don't go telling your friends you all can have small sips of alcohol. It's a cultural thing." Zoya quipped as she finished her drink.

Aalia leaned back in her chair. "I have been drinking since I was in diapers."

"Caribbean kids rule!" Marlene poured herself a new glass of wine. "This is what we are going to do. We will see how the investigation plays out. I think I can find out who the accuser is from Mr. Walker. We have a whole unfiltered relationship."

Aalia's demeanor perked up. "That is what I am thinking too. Once we know who the accuser is, we can really see how the investigation can turn out."

Chapter 11

JASMINE AND CRAIG SAT in Mr. Walker's office. Craig tried his best to keep Jasmine in a calm space. They stared at Mr. Walker as he read their complaint. Jasmine's fingers tapped against her purse. "How long is this investigation going to take? I intend on pressing charges. We came to you telling you that Mrs. Jimenez was harassing our son, she wasn't a fit teacher, and we have issued several complaints about her and now she is making our son feel uncomfortable. How many other students have complained about her being inappropriate? You just sweep things under the carpet. We should hold you responsible as well. You took none of our concerns seriously."

Mr. Walker looked up at Jasmine. "I am sorry that you feel this way, and I am deeply concerned not only for the welfare of your son but all the children. An outside party is conducting the investigation and Mrs. Jimenez was put on administrative leave. She has no access to any of the students and is not allowed on campus. I don't know how long the investigation will take, but please, when the investigators reach out to you, you must speak with them and provide any documentation you deem fit."

"I want her fired!"

"Mrs. Wright, the investigation results will determine if Mrs. Jimenez needs to be terminated. Right now, she is innocent until proven guilty."

Craig looked at Jasmine giving her a calm down nod. "Are there other kids who have been affected, did you even reach out to see if this affected anyone other than our son?"

Mr. Walker clasped his hands as he leaned back in his chair. "We are looking into it. We have to. Some concerned parents have come forward to ask questions, and one child has brought some allegations to our attention. Again, this all has to go through the investigation. I can't release any names or details just as I am not doing that about your son to others."

"Our son has felt uncomfortable in her class for a while but we did not know she was approaching him in this fashion. She is a grown ass woman and Chance is a child. He is trying to graduate and all this time Mrs. Jimenez was using her authority over him. We told you that she was treating him harshly and now it makes sense. If she wasn't getting what she wanted from him then that was her way to punish him. Do you know how traumatic this has been? He was keeping this to himself all this time. He was at his breaking point when he finally told Mrs. Carter. Shame on all of you!" Jasmine shot up from her chair, visibly rattled and agitated, her hands shaking as she clutched the purse straps. "If you all don't want to handle Mrs. Jimenez, I will."

Craig watched Jasmine rush out of Mr. Walker's office. "You understand why she is so upset?"

Mr. Walker came from around his desk. "I totally understand and I am so sorry this is happening."

Craig left Mr. Walker's office and walked out to the parking lot. He walked past the cars already lined up in the pick-up line. School wouldn't be out for another two hours, but parents would get to the school early. He waved at one of the parents then crossed the street to get to the parking lot. He could see Jasmine's arms flaying about as she must be on the phone and was riled up by the conversation. She could still be agitated from the meeting with Mr. Walker. Craig opened the door and got into the car.

Jasmine continued her conversation. She put on her seatbelt, then put her purse on the floor between her feet. "Let me get this clear, you are having an open house this weekend? Will she be there or are you having the sellers leave the house?" As soon as the car started, her Bluetooth was activated.

Brent's voice came in loud and clear. "This weekend. The sellers will be out of the house. You should come and see the property. You may have some clients who may be interested."

"Oh, I am definitely going to pass through. That is a very nice neighborhood and it's not far from us. There are so many positive selling points. What's the address again?"

"The address is 1609 Fishers Court."

"Thanks, Brent. See you Saturday." Jasmine looked at Craig with an amused grin. She stomped her feet happily. "Guess who is having an open house?"

"The guy you were talking to?"

"That's Brent."

"Oh, Brent, Brent!"

"Yes!" Jasmine squealed with joy. "But guess who the seller is?"

Craig concentrated on the road ahead of him. "I wouldn't even know how to guess."

"Mrs. Jimenez. That dumb bitch!"

Craig now realizing all the excitement Jasmine was exhibiting shook his head. "No, you are not going to be nosey in her house."

"Oh yes, I am. You heard Brent, I need to go see the property so I can see if I have any potential buyers. That neighborhood is great, close to good schools and very family-friendly. Yes, sir, I will be there. She won't be there and if she was I would be cordial."

"Small world. So her realtor is Brent McGregor. Wow!"

"Oh, this is going to be great. I am so excited. You just don't even comprehend how excited I am."

Chapter 12

••••

JASMINE SAT IN HER car around the corner from Mrs. Jimenez' house. She watched her leave and saw Brent drive into the cul-de-sac. She gathered her things and got out of her car. She yelled out to Brent and waved. She reached the end of the driveway where Brent was waiting for her. "I got here early."

Brent gave Jasmine a quick hug. "Come on so I can show you the place. I need to set up my displays and I got fresh baked cookies."

"I brought a nice vanilla essence to put in the oven. We will have the house smelling great in no time. I want a cookie." Jasmine took the tray of cookies as she observed Brent entering the lockbox code. They entered the home as Brent yelled a few hellos to see if anyone was there.

Brent took the tray of cookies from Jasmine and directed her to the kitchen. "You know I was in a vacant house the other day, I shouted greetings and silence. Then I am just setting up in the kitchen and I turn around and there is this huge dude behind me. I about punched him but he backed up and said he was the seller. He's lucky he didn't catch these fists. Then he left. The house is vacant and of all the days for him to show up is when I am there to show his house. Why was he even there?"

"That is so crazy. Something similar happened to me last month. You never know what to expect. There are also some nut sellers out there too." Jasmine placed the vanilla essence in a ceramic bowl and popped it in the oven turning the heat on low. "Make sure you remember to turn off the oven and remove the vanilla."

"I am adding that to my exit checklist. Thank you so much. I really appreciate that. Grab a cookie, and let's take a quick walk around. The open house doesn't start for an hour."

Jasmine followed Brent to the deck from the kitchen. She looked over the deck railing down into the pool. "Oh, a pool. How nice." She quickly decended the steps for a better look. The yard was very spacious, featuring a shed in the back of the lot-very nice indeed. As she walked further back she noticed the fire pit and grill. "This is a lovely yard."

"Isn't it? Let me show you the living space." Brent escorted Jasmine back up the deck stairs and through the kitchen to the living room. "Open floor plan, lots of natural light, gas fireplace, and we got three bedrooms upstairs with two full bathrooms. Downstairs, there is a bedroom or office and a full bathroom. Oh, and we got a two-car garage. Let's go upstairs." They both ran up the stairs going from room to room.

Jasmine took in the floor plan, asking questions sporadically. "I think I have a family perfect for this house. They have been looking for a couple months so far. Nothing has really caught their eye, but this could be a contender." After the tour, Jasmine stayed to help Brent set up. She looked out the window and could see people ready to view the house. "How are you handling crowd control? You want me to help and keep an eye on folks?"

Brent put an arm around Jasmine's shoulders. "That is so sweet of you. If you don't mind. You don't have to stay the whole time either. You know folks come in waves."

"I don't mind." Jasmine stepped aside so Brent could open the door and let people in. A young couple, a family of three, and Zoya and Marlene came into the home. Brent greeted everyone and recognized Zoya and Marlene. "Hey, recess parents! Jazz, look who is here."

Jasmine greeted the two families, letting Brent go off with them. "Ladies, are you looking for a new home?"

Zoya and Marlene laughed. "No, we are just being nosey. We live in this neighborhood."

"Shut up! Are you serious?" Jasmine ushered Marlene and Zoya into the living room. "Guess whose house this is?" Without giving them time to answer, Jasmine grabbed both of their arms in amusement. "Mrs. Jimenez."

Zoya and Marlene looked at each other in astonishment. "Get out!" Zoya's need to be nosey increased. "Girl, show us everything."

Marlene followed them to the kitchen then to the deck. They found themselves out on the deck and quickly scampering down the steps to talk. "So have you heard anything about the investigation?"

Jasmine waved her hand. "I can't stand that woman and she has been making my son very uncomfortable."

Zoya put her hand over her mouth. "Chance filed the complaint?"

"I have been complaining to Mr. Walker for months about Mrs. Jimenez and then to find out Chance was holding this information from me and his father. My heart is breaking. How dare she? I told Mr. Walker that she was using her authority to hamper my son and now I know that she was basically punishing him. I told Mr. Walker." Jasmine's voice became strained as she fought back tears.

Zoya and Marlene huddled around her, comforting her. "This is so disturbing. The investigation will show the truth and Mrs. Jimenez will get terminated. Whatever the outcome is, her teaching days are over."

Marlene looked at Zoya then they backed away to give Jasmine some space Jasmine got herself together. "You all want to see the rest of the house?"

Chapter 13

• • • •

JASMINE FLIPPED THROUGH Chance's yearbook stopping at the page with all of the teachers' pictures. She flipped the page, staring at Noemi Jimenez' photo. She started to see red. She put the yearbook on the passenger seat and got out of her car. She had a bit of a walk to do and she was determined to get her steps in for the day. Her thoughts quickly turned back to Mrs. Jimenez. This woman has been a nuisance since the first week of school. Jasmine had crossed paths with Mrs. Jimenez a few times and knew she lived nearby, but the fact that she was so close felt like a delightful flower in a garden of dismay. Jasmine didn't think things through; she was angry-no she was beyond angry. The school failed her and her son. She did her due diligence and reported each incident and what did the school do with that? Dismissed her, disregarded her concerns, and allowed Mrs. Jimenez to go unchecked. Jasmine's sole purpose was to protect her son.

Jasmine continued walking into the neighborhood passing, the Elementary school and making her way to Fisher's Court. Although it was still very warm, it was now getting dark. Jasmine had her ball cap on then pulled her hoodie over that. No plan, no guidance, just determination pushed her forward. She confidently entered the cul-de-sac, saw Mrs. Jimenez's car in the driveway, ran up the steps and was about to knock on the door. She looked down at the lockbox and entered the code she saw Brent enter. She retrieved the key and unlocked the door then put the key back in the lockbox. She pushed the door open quietly and slowly. She looked about the front entrance and heard the deck door slide open. She tiptoed to the kitchen and peered around the archway. Nobody was there but someone was on the deck. Jasmine entered the kitchen, heading to the sink where there was a window. She peeped out the window and saw Mrs. Jimenez leaning against the deck rail. Jasmine took in a measured breath as she got more and more pissed off. The deck door was never closed and Jasmine rushed out onto the deck. She crossed the deck quickly and grabbed Mrs. Jimenez' ponytail, dragging her down to the floor.

Jasmine and Noemi tussled for a few minutes. Noemi pushed the heel of her hand into Jasmine's chin then pushed her off. Noemi was so confused and couldn't get her bearings. She just kicked and punched haphazardly. She could feel her foot make contact with Jasmine. She quickly got up and tried to run to the door. Jasmine yanked her back, pulling her by the arm and pushing her. Jasmine grabbed an owl head shaped candle from the table, the hot wax splashing on her hand. She stepped forward, her hand sprang forward and threw the candle at Noemi. She watched the candle which was slightly bigger than a softball, hit Noemi in the face.

Noemi grabbed her face as blood poured from her now broken nose. She staggered back until her lower back hit the deck rail. Jasmine ran at Noemi, pushing her over the deck. She heard Noemi hit the ground with a thud then looked over the railing at her. Jasmine turned and ran down the steps. She stood over Noemi who was not fully with it and in a lot of pain. Jasmine watched Noemi go unconscious. She grabbed her, her hands cupping Noemi's armpits. She dragged her to the pool, then put her down. She looked at her briefly then pushed her into the pool. Noemi went under the water and didn't come up. Jasmine walked over to the gate, unlatched it and let herself out. The gate automatically locked behind her. She left the cul-de-sac and calmly made her way back the way she had come. She started to panic. What had she done? No turning back now. Mrs. Jimenez got what she deserved. She looked at her smart watch as it congratulated her for accomplishing all of her steps. She quickened her pace as she saw her car. She got into her car and her phone rang. She picked it up. "Hey, Chance."

"Mom, can we have pizza? Where are you?"

"Oh, I will get the pizza. I was viewing a house for a client. I will be home soon." Jasmine pulled down her hoodie and took off her ball cap. She fiddled with her bangs then started the car. She looked at herself in the rearview mirror and smiled.

Chapter 14

• • • •

ZOYA AND AALIA WERE driving back home after having a dinner date. Aalia checked her messages then started to watch a video. "You said Mrs. Jimenez lives in our neighborhood?"

"Yes, remember I was going with Marlene to the open house we got the flyer for? Well that's her house. It is a lovely house. Similar floor plan to ours, but her back yard faces the tree line. There are no houses behind hers and the other two houses in the court kind of face the entrance to the cul-de-sac."

Aalia's face brightened with realization. "Oh she lives back there. Nobody goes back there."

"I will show you the house." Zoya crossed the intersection and turned into the neighborhood. She passed the school and headed deeper into the neighborhood. They pulled up to the cul-de-sac seeing a fire truck and an ambulance. Zoya put the car in park and hopped out of the car. She ran up to the people standing in front of Mrs. Jimenez's house. "What's going on?"

An older lady with her hand over mouth turned towards Zoya and Aalia. "Not too sure, but I heard the husband yelling about Noemi being in the pool. Oh, it was a fright hearing him scream like that."

Zoya looked at Aalia then they stood with the onlookers and watched them bring Noemi from the backyard and put her in the ambulance. Zoya looked at Aalia "What the hell?"

Aalia was unmoved as she watched the scene before her, then she felt warm tears streaming down her face.

"Oh, let's go. You don't need to witness this." Zoya put her arm around Aalia, drawing her in close and walked her back to the car. They sat in the car as the emergency vehicles rushed out. "She will be all right."

• • • •

CHANCE STACKED TWO slices of pizza on top of each other and proceeded to eat. He looked at his mom who seemed very distracted. "You all right?"

Jasmine turned quickly to look at Chance. "Yeah, I am great. I have some titles I need to work on. I will be in my office." Jasmine walked to her office that she shared with Craig. She went out onto the wrap around deck and hugged herself as the air started to get a little chilly. She stood there staring and listening. It was eerily quiet, not even bug sounds could be heard. She put her hand on her stomach where Mrs. Jimenez landed a good kick. She lifted her hoodie up and could see the bruise. She let out a quick whistle as she lifted her arm and could feel pain in her shoulder. She spun around and closed the door behind her. She left the office and went to start a hot bath. She threw in a few handfuls of Epsom salt and some of her favorite bubble bath. The bathroom soon smelled of lilacs. She put the toilet seat down so she could sit down. She watched the tub fill and the bubbles multiply. She quickly stripped off her clothes and hopped in the tub. She really enjoyed her soaker tub. As soon as the hot water touched her stomach she winced but kept lowering herself in.

She looked at her smart watch seeing a flurry of messages pop up. She tapped her watch to call Zoya. "What's up, Zoe?"

"Jazz, you would not believe what has happened. Mrs. Jimenez was in a terrible accident. She was found in her pool by her husband."

Jasmine pushed herself upright. "What? How do you know this?"

"I was driving home and decided to show Aalia where Mrs. Jimenez lives. We got there and the ambulance was there. I was talking with one of the neighbors and they said they heard the husband screaming. Not too much details, but when they brought out Mrs. Jimenez, I saw the husband and he was soaked. She must have been found in the pool."

"An accident?" It wasn't a question but Jasmine had to go along with the story.

"Yes, an accident. Again, I don't have full details."

"Okay, thanks for letting me know. I guess. If you hear anything let me know. That is so unfortunate." Jasmine ended the call as Craig opened the door, presenting her with a tray to fit across the tub with a couple slices of pizza and a glass of wine. Jasmine smiled at Craig as she reached for her glass of wine. She took a long sip. "I made all of my steps today."

"You got in 10,000 steps? Cool. I have been slacking. Thanks for picking up the pizza."

"All in a day's work, my dear." Jasmine used her free hand to grab a slice of pizza.

Chapter 15

• • • •

AALIA STRAIGHTENED her shirt before taking her seat next to Sophie. She had a rough night and didn't get much sleep. Her thoughts kept going back to Mrs. Jimenez. Everything was a blur but seeing Mrs. Jimenez on the stretcher and being put into the ambulance was clear. Aalia picked at her salad, her appetite gone. "You should have seen her, Sophie. It was horrible."

Sophie devoured her lunch and tapped her fork against Aalia's salad. "You eating that?"

Aalia slid her salad over to Sophie then turned as she heard Brent arguing with Chance. She watched Brent defend himself, his friends stepping in behind him for support. It seemed he had finally had enough of Chance's jerky behavior. Soon a scuffle broke out, prompting the lunchroom aides to rush over and break it up. Mr. Walker who was walking past the cafeteria quickly assessed the situation and took Chance with him to his office.

Sophie finished the salad and dabbed at her mouth with her napkin. She gathered both trays and went over to the trash bins. She dumped the trash and placed the trays on the tray cart. She returned to her seat to pass the remaining 15 minutes left in lunch. "Aalia, Mrs. Jimenez will be fine. There is nothing you can do so stop beating yourself up. You are stressing out over things that are out of your control and not really your concern."

"She could have died." Aalia stared at the table.

"It was an accident. Nobody knows what is going on."

Aalia shook her head, acknowledging she was assuming too much. "I just feel bad for her."

Sophie grabbed Aalia's hand. She gave it a quick reassuring squeeze. "Just pray for her and Mr. Jimenez." The girls got up to head out to recess. Sophie waved at her mother as they stepped through the door.

Marlene reached out for Aalia. "Are you doing all right?"

"Still upset from last night."

Marlene surveyed the blacktop, monitoring the kids. "Mrs. Jimenez should be fine. Mr. Walker got an update from Mr. Jimenez. She is in a coma, but it was a medically induced coma. They are monitoring her."

Aalia went to sit down on the bench. Her stomach was unsettled. She leaned forward, feeling nauseous. "This isn't right. Something is not right with this whole thing."

Chapter 16

• • • •

CRAIG LOOKED AT CHANCE, disappointment etched on his face. "Why do you bother that boy? Leave him alone. What is your issue with him?"

"I don't have an issue with him."

"You must have an issue if you keep interacting with him and now you are suspended. You are harassing that boy every chance you get."

"Dad."

"Don't try to deflect. This is not the first time I have been called to your school. Fighting in the cafeteria this time, last time you were antagonizing him and the lunch aids had to send you to the office. There are too many people who witness your behavior and can corroborate what Brent is saying. Just leave him alone. He is not bothering you, you leave him alone. Honestly, you have bigger issues."

Chance watched his father walk away, heading to the garage to tinker with one of his cars. Chance darted around the sofa, running down the hall to his mother's office. He stood at the door, watching her stare out of the window. She had been acting weird the past couple of days. She seemed skittish and jumpy. He walked in slowly as not to startle her. "Mom." He watched her quickly turn her head to stare at him. "Is everything alright?"

Jasmine turned her head back to look out the window. "I'm good." She wasn't too sure if she was, but she may as well talk it into reality. She dragged her hands against her thighs. She looked at her hands, a bruise on her knuckles and a few scratches. "I need to get your ass back in school. You are a senior. This is not the time to be suspended."

"It's just a few days, and I have all my assignments. I will work on them and turn them in when I go back."

"That is not the point! You are a senior. Of all the time to just be focused and we have to deal with this crap."

"At least Mrs. Jimenez is not teaching me anymore."

"According to Mr. Walker, you are still on a fine thread. You need to get back on track, turn in your work and make sure you graduate on time."

"I will, Mom. Don't worry about it." Chance reached for his baseball hat. "What is this doing in here?"

Jasmine smiled at Chance then went back to staring out the window. "I borrowed it."

• • • •

ZOYA AND MARLENE STOOD at the door, listening to the chirping birds and the whirring of lawnmowers in the background, while one of the neighbors tended to her garden. The door flew open and Mr. Jimenez waved them both in. Juan closed the door behind them leading them to the sitting room. "Thank you for coming over. It has been hectic around here."

Zoya handed Juan a bouquet of flowers as Marlene placed a casserole on the coffee table. "How is Noemi doing?"

Juan's gaze dropped as he took in an exhausted breath. "Still in a coma. She is hanging in there. The doctors are really trying to piece things together. She had some head trauma, and they think she fell off the deck or stumbled down the stairs and, in her confusion, fell into the pool."

"Are the police involved?" Zoya's palms started to sweat.

Juan got up to get waters for everyone. "Do you all like ice in your water?"

"We are fine with whatever you got." Marlene nudged Zoya.

Juan quickly came back with three glasses of ice-cold water. "Here you go. To answer your question, the police are looking into it but no leads yet. It could just be an accident. My neighbors didn't see anything out of the ordinary and of the two neighbors, one was out of town. The police are waiting for Noemi to wake up and see if she remembers anything."

"That totally makes sense." Zoya's eyes scampered about the room gathering as much info as she could. "I never knew you all lived in the neighborhood until that night. Small world, huh?"

"Yes, we have been back here a good decade now."

"We couldn't leave you hanging. We can help out any way we can."

Juan looked at the casserole. "This is really nice of you. You didn't have to. I really appreciate the outpouring from the school and my neighbors. I don't feel alone…if that makes sense?" Juan took a long sip of his water. "With this misconduct allegation at the school and us looking to move, it has been a lot."

Marlene wiped her brow with the back of her hand. "How is that going? The investigation?"

"Oh really, it is going nowhere. I guess they are meeting with potential witnesses. Other than the allegation being brought to Noemi's attention from Mr. Walker, we haven't heard much. Then this happens. I think this is just a ruse. They are trying to make Noemi out as a scapegoat. I don't know for what, but I know my wife. She is not interested in any of her students."

Zoya and Marlene shared a glance then turned back to Juan with pleasant smiles on their faces. "Do you at least know who the student is?"

"Oh no, they won't release that tidbit of information. Protecting their privacy they say. It's bullshit. Let us know who is accusing her of inappropriate behavior. What is the inappropriate behavior? Which reminds me I need to get an attorney. I really am just focusing on her recovery. All this other stuff can kick rocks."

Zoya finished her water. "You know my husband is an ER doctor. He was on duty when your wife came in but he was treating another patient."

Juan looked at his phone, seeing Brent's name pop up. "I have to take this. I will be right back."

Zoya tapped Marlene on the knee. "I wonder if any of the neighbors have those ring cameras?"

"I wasn't really paying attention. We can get a better look when we are leaving."

"Just seems suspicious, right?"

"Yes, head trauma. Ooooh, you can have your husband look into it."

"No! He could get in trouble."

"He can figure a way out. He can just inquire."

"Marlene, don't get me started. I will talk to him. He will be off the next few days. He has really been putting in mad hours."

Juan walked back into the sitting room. "That was my realtor, apparently, a family wants to see the house. I usually clear out and let them do their thing. They will be here in about 15 minutes. I got to cut this short. Maybe we can meet up again. I am going to go check on Noemi."

Zoya and Marlene said their goodbyes and exited the house. As they walked down the steps and to Marlene's car they gave the two other houses in the cul-de-sac a look over. No ring cameras, not even a security light. They nodded at each other as they got into the car.

Chapter 17

• • • •

ZOYA SAT ON THE BED, wrapped in her robe with a T-shirt on her wet hair. She tied the shirt around her hair and just sat there. She could hear Aalia having a conversation with Sophie. Her door flung open as Leonard strolled in, tossing his sneakers on the ground then making his way over to the loveseat by the bookcase. "What's up, Doc?"

Leonard smiled mostly to himself as he wrung his hands together. "I am glad to be home. It has been a rough week in the ER."

Zoya pulled the T-shirt from her head, testing the dampness of her hair. She tossed the T-shirt into the hamper. She stared at Leonard, knowing he was going to be tired of her antics. "I was wondering if you knew anyone in the ICU?"

"I know a few people in ICU, I was just up there checking in on an ER patient."

Zoya sprang to her feet, scampering across the room to join Leonard on the loveseat. "Please tell me it was Noemi Jimenez."

"Jimenez? No, I was looking at Ms. Chang." Leonard looked at Zoya suspiciously. "You want information on Mrs. Jimenez?"

"Yes, is she okay? What is a medically induced coma? Does she just wake up? What is this head trauma Juan mentioned?"

"Who the hell is Juan?"

"Juan is Noemi's husband. Keep up." Zoya giggled as she tried to maintain her composure.

"How do you know her husband?"

Zoya started laughing hysterically as she looked at Leonard's exasperated expressions. "I know you are not with my antics but listen. Marlene and I…"

"Marlene is in this, too? Of course she would be. Why am I not surprised?"

"Yes, Noemi lives in the neighborhood. So we kind of connected with Juan, and Marlene made a casserole and we dropped it off."

"Oh, Lord! So, to answer your long-winded nosey questions. Noemi was placed in a medically induced coma so she can heal. She was the drowning victim right? She probably wasn't breathing for a long time, and they brought her back, but her body is still in shock. She is on a ventilator to help her breathe. To get her out of the coma, she will be weaned off the medication that was used to put her in the coma. They probably have scanned her brain to see if there is any long-term damage. I don't know the details, but when the doctors feel they can start to let her wake up, they will. As for the head trauma, I didn't really look at her but from when she was in the ER, she had a broken nose."

"So who is her doctor?"

"There is a staff of ICU doctors, she gets seen by whoever is on duty at the time."

"Maybe you can check with her doctors."

"For what?"

Zoya smirked. "I mean I can go back to Juan and inquire but I don't want to be that person. You just tell me."

"Have you heard of HIPAA?"

"This is me, I am not going to do anything crazy with the information."

"You are going to run right to Marlene with any information you hear."

"Come on, she is our kid's teacher. Oh my goodness. You won't get in trouble."

"You're right, I won't get in trouble because I am not going to even let myself fall into this trap. Robert is coming over, he is one of the ICU doctors. Maybe, just maybe while I am firing up the grill you may overhear some conversation. I am just saying."

Zoya jumped up from her seat, doing a little dance, then she grabbed her phone off of the dresser. "So Angelica will be here with Robert?"

"Yes, they will be here to hang out."

Zoya had to plan on how she was going to gather all of this information without looking desperate or suspect.

Chapter 18

• • • •

BRENT SR. PARKED HIS car behind Jasmine's car. He was going back and forth with Mr. Walker over how they would handle an event the school was going to hold. Somehow he needed to find time to help build backdrops. He exited his car, hustling over to assist Jasmine with placing the for-sale sign in the yard. "Looks like you don't need my help."

Jasmine dusted off her hands on her jeans. "I can always use your help. Not like we work with rival realtors."

Brent Sr. took a look around the neighborhood. "I mean my office is doing pretty well. We haven't been overlapping with your group too much." Brent followed Jasmine into the house she was going to be showing. He started to look around, investigating the property. "Anybody home?" he whispered.

"No, they are out. They left about half an hour ago." She pointed to the kitchen. "Grab a cookie."

Brent didn't need to be told twice. He made his way to the kitchen island, grabbing a cookie and a bottled water. The sweet scent of Jasmine's signature vanilla wafted through the air. He glanced at her sign-in book and the neatly arranged business cards on the counter. Typical perfectionist. He went to the side room, noticing a beeping noise. He rounded the corner, seeing someone standing by the fireplace. He could have sworn Jasmine said nobody was home. He walked over his hand extended for a handshake. "Hi, I am Brent McGregor...What are you doing here?"

Chance put his phone in his pocket. He took a step back but continued to stare at Brent. "I am here with my mom, being suspended and all, she thought I could be of some help."

"You are Jasmine's son! Well, I guess you wouldn't be suspended if you weren't messing with my son." Brent quickly turned to see where Jasmine was then turned back to Chance. "I will fuck you up. Don't even look at my son." Brent grabbed Chance's hand bringing him close as he patted him on the shoulder. He turned around as Jasmine walked in.

Jasmine smiled broadly. "Is this your first time meeting my Chance?"

"Yes, yes, it is. I never in my wildest dreams placed this young man with you."

"Oh Brent, you aren't at the school as much as I am. You are busy building your real estate empire."

"Well, I am making more of an effort to be at the school. Good to meet you, Chance."

Chance shook his head quickly then left the room.

"Well, Jasmine, I think you are good here. Have a good open house."

"Wait, how are things with the Jimenez house?"

"Oh, that is going as well as expected. Lots of foot traffic. Matter of fact I was just over there with a family. They are thinking of putting in an offer."

"Where are the Jimenez family looking to move to?"

"They haven't found a home yet. There is a contingency in place for them to have a month to move out. Anything could change of course. You never know with buyers."

"Understood. I see a car has pulled up. I will update you on any progress with this house."

Chapter 19

MARLENE AND ZOYA HUDDLED around Mr. Walker as they watched the track team doing their thing. There was a school fundraiser quickly approaching and Marlene graciously volunteered for Zoya to be on the committee. There was a casino night theme, raffle tickets to be sold, decorations to be made and backdrops to be built. Marlene cheered on the boys as they ran past. "Mr. Walker, last year's event was very successful. I think we will do very well this time around. Who doesn't like casino night?"

Mr. Walker offered Marlene a warm smile. "Last year we made close to one hundred eighty thousand dollars. I was so impressed with everyone, and I think we can have a repeat performance this year."

"I really enjoy getting to dress up and hang with the other parents."

"Parents need a night out, too."

Marlene watched Mr. Walker venture off to meet the kids at the finish line. He was going to take a picture with the winner. He really did enjoy his photo opportunities and never missed a chance to be in a picture. Marlene reached in her backpack, pulling out two sandwiches, handing one to Zoya. "So, I wonder if Jasmine will show up to the fundraiser?"

"I don't see why not. She's not allowed on campus just yet, but Mr. Walker is not going to turn away a paying parent from the school fundraiser."

"There are already a lot of great items for the silent auction."

"I always bid on the wine and spa packages." Zoya clapped as the first-place runner crossed the finish line. Her gaze looking back over the hill to see the incoming runners. "The weekends go by too fast. Back to the grind tomorrow."

"Don't remind me. What are you going to do with the rest of your day?"

Zoya shook her bell as she saw Aalia racing towards the finish line. "Second place! That's what I'm talking about. Go girl!" Zoya and Marlene walked over to congratulate Aalia. Mr. Walker was already standing next to Aalia so a picture could be taken. Mr. Walker was such a photo whore. "I am not doing anything else today. I just want to take a nap and eat leftover lasagna."

"That sounds like a good idea I am going to work on more decorations for the fundraiser but before that, I need to get ready for the used uniform sale."

"If you see a skort sized 12."
"I got you!"

Chapter 20

••••

MARLENE LOOKED AROUND the used uniform storage room, she grabbed a rack of skorts. She made sure everything was arranged just so and looked neat. She couldn't stand a messy display of anything. Once everything looked right, she pulled two skorts, placing them in her tote bag for Aalia. She gave the room one more look over then headed out, closing and locking the door behind her. She walked down the hall to return the keys to the front office. A stream of first graders ran down the hall past her, their teacher yelling for them to stop running.

Marlene slowly opened the office door and tossed the key onto the secretary's desk. She could hear Mr. Walker getting animated; his naturally loud voice made it easy to overhear the conversation. Her curious nature took over as she walked closer to his office door. She stood silently listening. Her foot softly tapped the door but she had to cover it up by knocking on the door. Mr. Walker put his hand over the phone telling her to come in. She quickly pushed the door open and stood in the doorway. Mr. Walker ended the call.

Marlene stammered for a reason why she was there, quickly remembering she was in the storage room. "Hey, Mr. Walker, how are you doing? I was just letting you know I put the key to the storage room on Rosie's desk."

Mr. Walker smiled broadly "Oh, how nice of you. I was just on the phone with Mr. Jimenez. Good news that I am going to share in a newsletter. Mrs. Jimenez should be coming out of her coma in the next few weeks. We must continue to keep her and her husband in our prayers for a speedy and full recovery."

"Oh, this is such great news indeed, Mr. Walker. I should get back to the pickup line." Marlene couldn't get out of the building fast enough. She saw cars already lining up. She walked over to the teacher's parking lot, quickly getting into her car and driving over to the end of the pick-up line. She was next to cone 14, the breeze blowing through her lowered windows felt good. She grabbed her water, taking a few sips and was pleased to get a few cold gulps down. She looked in her rearview mirror at Zoya who was pulling up behind her. She put her hand out her window waving at her to come join her. She unlocked the doors. "Zoya! Get in here!"

Zoya put her water bottle in the cup holder as she sat down and closed her door. "What's up?"

"Mrs. Jimenez is being brought out of her coma."

"Are you serious? That is great news. I was asking Leonard about her, and he says it can take a few weeks for her to be weaned off the medication they have her on. It is good to hear they are starting that process. I hope she has a speedy recovery. The kids will be glad to hear this news."

"Yes, Mr. Walker will send out a newsletter. I kind of heard his conversation with Juan. Okay, I was totally eavesdropping. Oh, here are the skorts you wanted." Marlene reached into her bag, pulling out the skorts and handing them to Zoya. "Size 12, right?"

Zoya clapped her hands enthusiastically before taking the skorts from Marlene. "Excellent. How much do I owe?"

"Paying it forward, don't worry about it."

Chapter 21

CHANCE FOLLOWED BRENT Jr. and his friends closely. He balled up his fist remembering how Brent's dad came at him. He wanted to punch Brent Jr. in the back of the head, but he just got back from his suspension and needed to behave himself. He continued on his way to the front door to escape the pull of the school. His pace picked up as he went to his dad's car. This month couldn't come to an end fast enough. He looked across the road, seeing Brent's dad having a good laugh as they waited for the cars in front of them to pull off. Brent Sr. had a huge truck and it was on oversized tires, making it more of a towering menace. Chance frowned as he tossed his backpack in the back seat. The air conditioner hummed as the car lurched forward. They would be home in ten minutes.

Chance stared out the window, suddenly tired. "Today was a day, Dad! I have no homework."

"That is good to hear. You can just relax."

"Are you and Mom going to the fundraiser?"

"I don't think I can go. I had your mom buy two tickets, but I may get there late. I was thinking you can drop your mom off, and when I get there I will bring her back home."

"Yeah, that is cool."

"Well, we have a couple weeks before the fundraiser. I will keep you posted."

"No problem." Chance stared at Brent Jr. as they pulled up next to them at the light. He gave him a slow middle finger with a smirk. Chance sunk into the seat as his father hit the gas pedal and sped off.

Chance unbuckled his seat belt before his father even pulled into the driveway. He watched the garage door open and reached for his backpack. As soon as he could, he got out of the car and walked into the house. The kitchen was flooded with sunlight. He grabbed an apple, took a bite, dropped his backpack by the breakfast table and ran downstairs to play his videogames with his friends. Someone had to be online. Chance looked toward the stairs, hearing his dad coming down. "What's up?"

"I just got a call, the investigator wants to talk to you about your interaction with Mrs. Jimenez."

Chance's heart beat quickened, his brow quickly gathering sweat. "Really?" His voice faded as he tried to think. How far was he going to take this? It was getting too real, too quick. "When do I have to talk to this investigator?"

"Tomorrow. They are coming here. I am going to have our attorney present. Let me give him a call now."

"Tomorrow after school?"

"Yup, if you want to stay home tomorrow you can. Get your mind right."

Chance put on his headphones, his game was about to start. He rocked his head side to side releasing the stress and tension that was building up in his neck. "No, I'm good. It's game time."

Chapter 22

JASMINE, CHANCE, AND Craig sat at the dining room table with Zachary, their attorney. Chance picked at his thumbnail, his breathing slow and calm. He could hear his parents talking to Zachary, but he wasn't comprehending their conversation. His mother was unusually calm, but he knew she would have a flare up, it was just a matter of time. Chance looked at the door when the doorbell chimed throughout the house. It was so quiet up until that point. A rush of air seemed to fill his ears blocking everything out. He watched his mom open the door and a tall woman step in, the sun shining behind her. Her braids pulled up in a neat bun. He watched her shake everyone's hands before stopping in front of him. Her warm brown eyes with flecks of green sparkled. He took her hand, warm and calm against his own. He smiled at her almost forgetting her reason for being there. "Hi, I am Chance." He quickly took his hand away, his face turning two shades of red.

"Hi, I'm Nicole and it is a pleasure to meet all of you. I wish it wasn't under these circumstances. If I may, I would like to speak with Chance. I understand that your attorney will be present." Nicole stood tall in her kitten heels and casual skirt suit.

"Can I speak to her alone, please?" Chance blurted the request. He watched his parents exchange looks between themselves then with Zachary and left to go sit in the kitchen. Chance pointed to the chair and sat down.

"As long as you feel comfortable." She pulled out her thermos, laptop, and a pair of rectangular glasses. "You had mentioned to the school counselor that Mrs. Jimenez had been inappropriate with you. Can you be more specific?"

Chance looked at the kitchen, he could see his father pacing back and forth and his mother's shadow by the entryway. "Mrs. Jimenez treats me differently. She comes down on me hard and for no good reason. I have complained to my parents, and they have brought it up to Mr. Walker. She keeps me after class when everyone has left, she says weird stuff. I don't know..." Chance fiddled with his thumb. "She told me she liked me and thought I was special. I didn't mind all of that, but it didn't feel right."

"Has there been any other incidents where you felt uncomfortable around Mrs. Jimenez?"

"She touched me! She tried to kiss me. I said no and ever since then she does everything in her power to make me look bad and it has come to the point where my ability to graduate is a question."

"Mrs. Jimenez's class is not the only class that has your ability to graduate on the line."

"Because of what she did to me and continues to do to me, has affected my ability to focus in other classes."

Nicole's fingers glided across her keyboard as if she was playing the piano. "You never mentioned her touching you or trying to kiss you to anyone until now?"

"I didn't want to get in any more trouble, I thought I could handle it. I was scared." Chance reached down to the deepest memory he had of his dog and let the tears stream down his face. "Mom!" he yelled.

Jasmine was already on her way to Chance's side. She wrapped her arms around him. "It's all right. We are going to press charges. I can't believe this."

Chance bit his lip as he leaned into his mother. He pulled his head up for air. "I should have told you, but I was scared. I didn't really understand what was going on. Ms. Nicole, you have to believe me."

Nicole reached for Chance's hand, giving it a quick squeeze. "I am so sorry, but you are telling us now and that is what matters."

Chance sat with Nicole for two hours relaying everything he could think of. He felt confident that she understood his point of view. Chance watched Nicole gather her things and explain what steps would follow. He excused himself to get a drink and sit on the deck. His composure returning, he really should have entered into one of the school's productions. He apparently had a knack for acting.

Chapter 23

••••

CHANCE UNPACKED THE car with some of the props his father built for the casino night fundraiser. He carried as much as he could over to the storage room in the gym. With the fundraiser only a few weeks away, there was a lot of building and painting going on. His dad was great with this kind of stuff. Chance helped and he enjoyed hanging out with his father. Chance propped the storage room door open with a chair then leisurely made his way over to a bunch of boys heading in for soccer practice. Chance walked into the boy's bathroom, running into Brent Jr. He stepped back then pushed past him.

Brent Jr. circled back following Chance. "I never did anything to you, but you keep being jerk. Anyway, you need help with the stuff in your car?"

Chance looked at Brent Jr. as he washed his hands. "Nah, I am almost done." Chance watched Brent Jr. leave. He raked his hand through his hair, making sure every strand of hair was laid just right. Chance finished drying his hands as he made his way back to the car. He dropped off the rest of the props his dad made and needed to get home. It didn't take long for him to get home. He was hungry and tired. He sat down, watching his father run into the kitchen.

"Where did you park? Did you see who hit you?"

Chance looked at his dad confused. "I wasn't hit by anyone?"

"Come." Craig led Chance to the garage. He circled the car to the passenger side. "Look at this!" Craig stood there, hands on his hips, his mouth agape.

Chance stepped around his dad, staring at a good-sized door ding and scrape marks one the back door. "Dad, I was only at the school to drop off the stuff for the fundraiser."

"You were in a parking space?"

"Yeah, but I mean, there wasn't a car by me. People were showing up for soccer practice."

"Some asshole must have side swiped the car and left knowing damn well they hit my car! Let me go see if I can get her into a body shop. Damn it."

"I am sorry..."

"Not your fault, there are assholes in the world."

Chapter 24

••••

JASMINE SURVEYED THE room with Brent Sr. "So what are you trying to do?" She followed Brent onto the deck, she confidently strolled over to the railing, looking down at the pool she tossed Noemi's body into. The pale blue water looked so enticing and inviting. "I thought you had a buyer for this property?"

"The deal kind of soured because the buyer had an issue with the pool. They have young kids and the liability."

"Why even look at a house with a pool if you know you don't want to have a pool?"

"You know buyers." Brent leaned against the railing. "I was thinking of having another open house, but I want it to be geared at a short list of potential buyers. Nothing too dramatic."

"What is the owner expecting?"

"Oh, Juan is hardly here so he is cool with it. He spends most of his time at the hospital, but his wife is coming out of the coma now."

"I see. Well, maybe you can get this property sold before the fundraiser."

"That is what I am hoping for. Juan has found the house he and his wife will move into so who wants to foot two mortgages. He will begin moving to the new house soon, there is some work he wants done before he moves in."

"Where is the new house?"

"Three miles up the road. You know the new development at Black Hills?"

"Nice. You will have some new neighbors."

"Yes, small world, right?"

"Small indeed."

"Well, I have to get going, but I will set up our guest list. I want you to pick some of your clients to view the home." Brent looked at his watch. "I have to get my truck detailed."

"Are you using the guy I told you about? He does more than detailing, he can do some body work too, if it's not too complicated."

"That's the guy I am going to see. Got to freshen the truck up a bit."

Chapter 25

••••

ZOYA GAZED LOVINGLY at Leonard, watching the gears turn in his head as he helped Aalia with her homework. She glanced at her tablet, where the cart was filled with items needed for the fundraiser. Peering over the tablet, she wondered if Leonard had any updates on Noemi. "Remember I told you Noemi was going to be waking up soon? Do you know how she is doing?"

Leonard grazed his chin with the back of his hand. He was busy working out the equation Aalia was working on. "Last I heard, she is doing well. They will try to determine what happened to her. You know they have to see what she remembers from that night."

"Oh that is good to hear. I hope she has a full and speedy recovery. You think it was an accident?"

"I don't know what to think. I am not up to speed on her case. Anything is possible. What we see in the ER can turn out very differently after the patient leaves. The things we see but we don't always get follow up."

"I hope Juan is doing well. I know he has got to be under a lot of pressure and stress. The sooner his wife is released from the hospital the sooner they can return to normal."

"Noemi is going to have some hills to climb after she is released. She will be all right, though."

Aalia wrapped up her homework, a long drawn-out yawn escaped from her mouth. "Are you two going to the fundraiser?"

"Your dad will be on call that night, but I am going with Marlene. You and Sophie can hang out."

"Maybe we can have a sleepover." Aalia puckered her lips, smelling the fruity fragrance of her lip gloss.

"We got a few weeks, once my order comes through, Marlene and I can really decorate the gym. It will be a lot of fun."

Aalia tapped away at her phone, texting Sophie and half listening to her mother. She looked over at her mother knowing Marlene was going to call her any second now.

Zoya looked at her phone then at Aalia. "You already invited Sophie over for a sleepover? We haven't agreed to a sleepover." Zoya watched Marlene's face appear on her screen. "These girls move fast."

Marlene laughed as her face came in and out of the screen as she walked about her kitchen. "They sure do. So is the sleepover cool? Can I sleepover, too. You know we are going to be drinking at the fundraiser."

"Oh my goodness, some parents were tore up drunk last year. Sure, let's just all crash over here." Zoya winked at Leonard who was probably glad he was going to be on call that night. He really wouldn't want to deal with all of them. She stared back at Marlene. "My order should be here by the end of the week. We will be ready to decorate the gym. What else do we need?"

"I am working with some other moms for catering. I think we have a menu set up and will finalize that in a week. What are you going to wear...we need to look nice."

"I haven't even thought of my outfit, but I am not wearing heels. Those days are over."

"I better not see you in some Queen Elizabeth 1900's."

"Shut up! Her shoes are doable. Low, block heels."

"Don't come around me looking like that. Stop it!"

"I am so done with you." Zoya could not contain the laughter that erupted from her mouth. She slapped her thigh as she fell on her side, her face buried in the couch cushion. "You did not say Queen Elizabeth 1900's. Why are you like this?"

Chapter 26

••••

CHANCE CHUCKLED TO himself as he watched Brent Jr. stumble around the gym. It was a hot day, and everyone was out running. A little hydration was needed by everyone. Chance took his water bottle that was full of a little alcohol concoction, and tossed the now empty bottle in the recycle bin. He looked at Brent Jr. double over and vomit violently. "The heat must have gotten to him." Chance tapped his friend's shoulder.

The gym teacher quickly ran over to check on Brent Jr. while yelling into his walkie talkie for the school nurse to get over there. Chance watched everyone rush over to Brent Jr., boy was he really sick. Chance had never seen so much vomit in his life. The janitor was not going to be happy. Due to the interruption all the kids were sent back to class. Chance made a quick pit stop at the bathroom before slowly heading back to class. His entire schedule was now thrown off. The school day passed without any further incidents, and he found himself at his cone waiting, for his dad to pull up. "Hey, Dad!" Chance got in the car quickly. "How is the car repair going?"

"Repairs will be done in a week. They have to fix the dents and of course paint the doors. I was actually trying to look at some of these parents' cars to see if the person who hit my car had any damage."

"Don't worry about it, Dad. I feel bad for the damage, but at least it was sort of a minor issue. It's the principle."

"Exactly! The person knows they hit the car and instead of owning up to it, they left." The rest of the ride home was silent, they both were thinking of food.

Chance scarfed down his food, put the plate in the dishwasher, grabbed his phone and made his way to his room. He started his gaming system and put his headphones on. Soon he was talking with a few of his friends. "Eric, wasn't today crazy?"

Eric chuckled. "What was going on with Brent Jr.?"

"I think the heat got to him."

"No, there was more to it. He was seriously sick. Mr. Walker was having an intense conversation with Brent Jr. and waving his water bottle around. I couldn't get a good listen because I needed to get back to class."

Chance cheered his friends on as they fought their enemies. "Interesting. I wonder what that was all about?"

"I guess we won't know."

Chance smirked, his eyes glued to the screen. He looked up at his father, standing in the doorway. "What's up?"

Craig motioned with his hand for Chance to mute his microphone. "I am heading to the liquor store. I need more vodka. My bottle was empty. I don't remember drinking that much. Anyway, you want anything while I am out?"

Chance gave his dad a thumbs up sign. "I am good. Thanks for asking."

Chapter 27

JUAN HELD NOEMI'S HAND, her palm's warmth stretching to his hand and fingers. He smiled at her as she smiled back at him. He gave her hand a loving squeeze while waiting for the nurses to come with the doctors. Noemi smiled through the pain and confusion that wrapped around her like a blanket. She could only whisper and say only a few words before the soreness of her throat clamped down on her.

Noemi closed her eyes as she tried to remember how she got here. From Juan, she learned that she had fallen into the pool after a fall, but she really didn't understand it all. There was no need for her to dwell on it because she still had a lot of healing to do. What didn't sit well with her was the thought that she could have tried to hurt herself. There was no way she would ever consider such a thing; that thought would never cross her mind, nor did she possess the physical ability to carry it out. It was simply not an option-now or ever.

Juan showed Noemi pictures of their new home. He had already started moving things over and hired a company to pack up the house for the final move. By the time Noemi came out of the hospital, she would be moved to the new house directly. His brows wrinkled as he described each room and the work that was being done. He was quite pleased with his choice and knew Noemi would agree. Noemi stared at the picture of the deck, she reached for her nose remembering she had injured her nose, she could feel the splint around her nose and winced at the thought that her nose was broken. She leaned back into her pillows, half listening to the attending doctor's instructions. She felt tired and was having a difficult time keeping her eyes open. She no longer saw the need to fight sleep. The doctor's voice faded as she drifted back to sleep. Whatever the doctor was saying was more for Juan than for her.

JASMINE SAT IN BRENT Sr.'s car, the cooling seat relieving her of the heat from her walk. Brent Sr. was busy having a one-sided conversation as he drove her to check out the Jimenez house. He was very proud of the sale and looking forward to sealing the deal on the old house.

Jasmine looked up at the house as they drove around the circle. They got out of the car just to walk around outside. "This is very nice indeed. I am glad you were able to close the deal."

Brent Sr. smiled at Jasmine. "I really like this neighborhood. There are three more house for sale here. Juan and Noemi should be moving in soon."

Jasmine's pulse quickened, she could feel a vein pulsating up her neck. "Soon? How soon?"

"Oh, you haven't heard? Noemi is awake. Juan has already started moving some things over, but a moving company will break everything down at the old house and get this house all situated."

"Oh, what good news. You would know about Mrs. Jimenez before anyone else. We will probably hear about her recovery in the school newsletter." Jasmine swallowed hard, she was disgusted by Noemi and based off of what Chance had told the investigator there was no way in hell she was going to let that slide. Jasmine made sure to file charges against her. As far as Jasmine was concerned, Noemi should have just stayed at the bottom of the pool.

Chapter 28

• • • •

BRENT SR. STOOD NEXT to his son, rocking back and forth on the balls of his feet. Together, they followed Marlene, Zoya, and Mr. Walker around the gymnasium to plot out where they wanted props, tables, and decorations to be placed. The Casino Night Fundraiser was around the corner. All the tickets had been sold and it was time to really get down to business. Brent Sr. watched Zoya and Mr. Walker veer off track and head to the far side of the gym. He stood next to Marlene as his son went off to talk to some friends.

Marlene stood in front of the basketball hoop, arms crossed over her chest. "How is Mrs. Jimenez doing?"

Brent Sr. lowered his gaze, looking at his sneakers. "She is doing well. They released her a few weeks back and she is getting accustomed to her new house."

"It was good to see she was released in the school newsletter."

"What a difference a few weeks can make, right?"

"Does she remember the night of her accident?"

"She still is foggy on that, but really she is more focused on her recovery." Brent Sr. matched Marlene's stance as she looked at her. "You know it was that Chance boy who made those allegations against her?"

Marlene's eyes opened wide with wonder and desire for more details. "Really, are you sure?"

"Definitely sure. Juan told me about 2 weeks ago. Charges were filed against her and the investigator spoke with him. You see, she needs to know who is accusing her of this and she had the right to know what she is being accused of. I only know because of Juan. It's not news that is out there like that so don't say anything. There is an ongoing investigation. Something is not right with that damn boy. He keeps messing with my child. You may not know but my son got very sick a few weeks back, and Mr. Walker said my son's water bottle smelled like it had alcohol in it. Now, my son has never had a drop of anything beyond sports drinks. I really believe that Chance kid spiked his water. I can't prove it, but I can feel it in my bones."

Marlene gasped in shock. "You are not the first parent to complain about Chance. My daughter is a couple grades behind him, but he seems to be problematic."

"All I know is that boy is going to cross the wrong kid and the wrong parent. I don't play when it comes to my kid. All bets are off, if you know what I mean?"

Marlene nodded in agreement. "I know you don't know the Jimenez family all that well, other than being their realtor, but do you think her accident was an accident?"

"You know I have thought about that a few times. I am not going to lie, it doesn't really add up. Even Juan can't explain what happened. He just doesn't see her falling in the pool or breaking her nose. How did she break her nose? How did she end up in the pool?"

"So many questions. Maybe they should have the police look into things."

"Maybe. I don't even know where to begin with that."

Marlene thought about it and was at a loss for what could be done. "Maybe the neighbors have security footage that may show something out of place."

Brent Sr. nodded his head at his son as he was making his way back to him. "Well, that is up to Juan and Noemi to look into it. Since she can't remember much details, I don't know how much she can even offer the police." Brent Sr. stretched out his arm to give his son a fist bump. "Ready to head home?"

Marlene said her goodbyes then wandered out of the gym to find Zoya. Zoya and Mr. Walker were still deep in conversation. Marlene winked at Zoya, signaling that she needed to wrap things up so they could start a much better discussion. She walked briskly to her car waiting for Zoya to join her. They were definitely in for an interesting ride home.

Zoya opened the back door to drop off empty boxes she would use to bring more of the props for the fundraiser. She quickly got into the passenger seat. "What is going on? I can tell you have tea to spill and me practically wearing all white."

"Okay, what I tell you can't go anywhere. This must stay with us."

Zoya's interest piqued with a fevered pitch. She clawed her thighs as she waited for Marlene to start divulging whatever it was that she knew.

Marlene started to drive off the campus, her eyes darting from left to right. "Chance is the accuser, now I don't know what he accused Mrs. Jimenez of, but he is the one who filed the complaint and whatever it was, has to be really egregious because charges were filed against Mrs. Jimenez?"

"Charges? Was she arrested?"

"I don't know, I didn't even think to ask all those questions. I did ask if Brent Sr. thought it was an accident." She made air quotes with her fingers then placed her hand back on the steering wheel. "Doesn't it just seem odd, all the injuries she had, how can that be an accident?"

"Interesting." Zoya could feel her heart pounding against her ribs. She lowered her window, as she was getting not just warm but hot and a bit bothered. "I am going to need a drink."

"Remember, not a word, not even to the girls."

"You have to find out what the allegations were, they won't release that information?"

"Well, maybe, I can get that from Brent Sr. when we are setting up the gym. Casino Night is going to be explosive."

"I think you mean lit. Casino Night is going to be lit!"

Marlene shrugged her shoulders. "I can't keep up with the hot slang of today's youth. Lit, what is lit?"

"It's definitely not literature."

Marlene snort laughed as she pulled up to Zoya's house. "Don't forget the boxes."

Chapter 29

••••

JASMINE SAT IN HER car after loading her groceries into the trunk. The windows slightly cracked, allowing a steady stream of air swirl past her. Brent Sr. had a calm but questioning voice that spilled effortlessly from her phone. This conversation was not reassuring to her but making her anxiety climb to new heights. "Okay, so what do you mean you don't think it was an accident? Why do you think you need to bring this up to Mr. Jimenez?"

Brent Sr. let out a slow sigh. He was feeling flustered. "Listen, that is why I am telling you. I am wondering if I should express my feelings about this to Juan. I just feel off about the whole thing."

"You and Juan are not friends. You were their realtor. Your job is done. You should not mention any of this to them. It is traumatizing, you hear me! How would you feel if some random guy came up to you and was like oh, I don't think your wife's injuries that had her in a coma, was an accident. You would look at him like who the fuck are you? Your job is done. Leave this alone." Jasmine could feel her heart pounding, she was infuriated and terrified all at the same time. She could see herself bashing Noemi in the face with whatever it was she picked up. She was wild, animalistic, and meant every bit of harm when she confronted Noemi that night. Hell, she didn't even confront her, she broke into her house and brutally attacked her. Her hands trembled upon the steering wheel, she didn't even realize she was gripping the steering wheel so hard. She scanned the parking lot watching people pass by. Out of the peripheral view she saw a car she recognized. She watched the car park and the person gingerly exit the car. "Are you serious, this bitch can drive and be out and about!"

"Oh, dang, what? What is going on, Jasmine? Who are you talking about?"

"Mrs. Jimenez just walked in the grocery store."

Brent Sr. still a little stunned with Jasmine's outburst chuckled. "Yes, she can drive. She has to return to her normal life. She has been out of the hospital for a few weeks now, remember?"

Jasmine gritted her teeth, her hand on the door handle ready to open the door, rush out and get in Noemi's face. She gathered her composure, but remained irritable. "Anyway, don't mind me. Speak of the devil and the devil shall appear. Where was I? Oh, yeah, don't say anything. Does she even remember what happened?'

"No, that is the thing, she doesn't have much memory."

"Okay, well you definitely should leave this alone. You going over there and telling them this nonsense could actually make things worse. Like you could implant information or memories that were never there. Then check this out, what if, what you say is proven to not be true, then the police are looking at you like you know more about the incident."

"Okay, true crimes lady. Damn. I won't say anything. Thank you for talking me off the edge. I will just keep the opinion to myself. How about that?"

"Good. Very good!" Jasmine tried to reassure herself that this would not go any further. She cautiously pulled out of her parking space and slowly drove a little past Mrs. Jimenez' car. She looked at the one bag of groceries she put on the passenger seat, took out two eggs and tossed them at the back windshield. She then grabbed her frappuccino, took the cover off and tossed that whole container at the car. Satisfied with her poor choices and bad decisions, she drove off. She brought down her sun visor and laughed. Let the sun bake that concoction onto the car. She turned up the air because today was a broiler type of day.

Chapter 30

BRENT SR. AND MARLENE stood with Zoya inside the gym, looking at all their hard work. Some other parents were still setting up the space for the fundraiser, but it was time for a break. Marlene shook her water bottle, the ice clanking within. She took a sip knowing there was no water in there but a good adult drink. "Guys, this looks amazing. We are going to have so much fun. The final touches are coming together."

Brent Sr. twisted his torso, stretching out his back as much as he could. "It is coming along. It's always fun to see Mr. Walker asking for money. This school sure as hell is not in the red."

"They just raised next year's tuition too." Marlene nudged Zoya as they watched the other parents.

"I am slightly peeved with that but this is my kid's last year."

"You think Mr. Jimenez will be present this year?"

"I haven't talked to him. After the sale of their house I haven't really spoken to either of them. I was advised that my job is done. It's not like we are friends."

"True. Also, Mrs. Jimenez can't be on campus."

"Oh, did I tell you what the allegation is? That kid said she kissed him and was coming on to him. He felt threatened and because he didn't want a relationship with her, she has been grading him differently and trying to ruin him educationally."

Zoya and Marlene both wide eyed, inched in closer to surround Brent Sr. "Say what now?" Zoya whispered.

"Yes, that is what the allegations are. I don't see her doing all of that, but that is why an investigation needs to be done. They have talked to other students, and it's a toss up. Some kids are like no, they never witnessed that, but a few kids are saying that the dynamic between the two was kind of off and not just because Chance is an asshole."

Zoya shook her head upon hearing Chance's name. "That child can be a menace from what I have heard from our daughters, and they are not in his grade."

"That is what I am talking about. He harasses my kid all the time. The school does basically nothing to reprimand Chance. I can't stand him."

Marlene finished her drink then looked at Zoya then Brent and back to Zoya. "Remember, don't say anything to anyone. This is an ongoing investigation." She watched Brent and Zoya nod in unison.

Chapter 31

• • • •

JASMINE AND BRENT SR. stood in the doorway to the gym, dressed to the nines and ready to participate in the school fundraiser. Casino Night was already off to a good start. Parents were participating in the silent auction, others were playing legit casino games and the house was definitely going to win. "Good job, Brent." Her eyes swept over the room, taking in everyone and everything. Spotting the bar, she made her way over with a spring in her step and tapped Zoya on the shoulder. "How many drinks have you had?" A toothy grin spread across her face.

"This is my third glass of Chardonnay. Marlene over here brought her own bottle."

Marlene giggled. "Hey, don't say that out loud. She brought some rum punch." Marlene pointed at Zoya's embroidered bucket purse.

"You two are not playing. Can I have some of the rum punch?" Jasmine reached for a cup and winked at Zoya. "Fill her up!"

The trio hung out and were definitely acting the fool the whole time. They were having a great time. They made their way to the silent auction tables, then played a few hands of poker. Jasmine turned from the table as she heard a commotion. People were huddled by the entrance and appeared to be in a tizzy. She tapped Zoya and pointed at the door. "I wonder what that is all about?" Jasmine sipped her drink finishing it in one last gulp. She could feel her chest burn and her face flush. She was a few drinks in by now and dinner hadn't even been served. She watched the crowd part and through the crowd strolled Noemi Jimenez. A few other teachers were with her walking in with her like some kind of power squad.

Zoya, sensing the distress, put a hand over Jasmine's clenched fist. "Breathe!"

"I'm good!" Jasmine screeched. "Why is she here?"

Zoya waved at Mr. Walker who appeared to see Jasmine's reaction and was already heading in their direction. Mr. Walker stood in front of Jasmine, blocking her view of Noemi. "I didn't know she was coming. Technically, there are no children here, but I will request that she leaves."

Jasmine released her fist and got up to get to her table. The food was being sent out. "Brent or Zoya, can one of you get a bottle of red wine sent to our table?" Jasmine left in a huff and found a seat. She started eating bread and stabbing at her salad with her fork. The bottle of wine arrived and she promptly poured her glass almost to the brim. She took a couple sips then got up to get some air. She walked the perimeter of the gym and strutted between a few tables until she could see Noemi. She watched her standing next to another teacher, tossing her head back in a fit of laughter. Jasmine felt the irritation burrowing more and more into her very soul. Her pace quickened and she pushed a parent to the side, pretended to trip, threw the glass full of red wine at Noemi's back and stumbled off as she heard Noemi gasp and the gaggle of women shriek.

Jasmine looked back long enough to see women trying to dab at the stain of wine covering Noemi's beige dress. Aww, too bad for her. Noemi rushed out of the gym and Jasmine watched her leave, feeling a sense of satisfaction that she had removed the trash from the event. She quickly went to the bar to get a new wine glass and went to her seat as if nothing had happened. She was too smooth with it. She stabbed at her salad again, a broad smile spread across her face.

Zoya looked at Jasmine, patting her hand. "You good?"

"Oh, I am fucking great!"

After a night of drinking and spending money, the evening was coming to a close. Jasmine was not feeling too confident on her ability to drive and had called Chance to come pick her up. She stood outside with Brent Sr. waiting. She wrapped her shawl around her shoulders even though she felt rather warm. She saw Chance pull up and unlock the doors. "Well, my chariot has arrived."

Brent Sr. looked at Chance, not impressed or amused. "Get home safe. Should he even be out this late?"

Jasmine reached for the door handle. "We live like right around the corner. He's fine. He needs nighttime driving practice anyway." She got in the car and was feeling very drowsy. "Thanks for picking your old mother up."

"Are you drunk? Do we need to have a talk?" Chance laughed. "I'm so going to tell Dad." There wasn't much traffic on the road, it was just a muggy evening. He looked in the rearview mirror, blinded by headlights that were on high beams too. The vehicle was coming up close so he switched lanes and the vehicle followed suit. "Are you serious right now?"

Jasmine half asleep, her body slumped forward then jerked hard to the right then the left, she instantly sat up as the car started to spin out of control. She looked at her son, the car went over the curb and down the hill, rolling into Lake Whetstone. Her head slammed into the dashboard. She never put her seatbelt on. Her body pressed up against the dashboard and windshield. She coughed and started to swallow water. She looked at Chance, his head against the steering wheel. All she saw was air bubbles swarming around her. Her eyes closed.

Chapter 32

••••

MARLENE THREW ON HER hazard lights and Zoya waved down other cars. They ran down the hill to get to the car that was now under water. Marlene and Zoya stood there, neither of them could swim. Another driver ran down the hill and quickly jumped into the lake. Marlene dialed 911 as more people rushed to the water to either watch or dive in to help.

Zoya grabbed Marlene's arm for reassurance. Together they watched one man come up with Chance and start to do CPR. Another man came up with Jasmine and he too started to do CPR. The ambulance arrived with a fire truck and several police cars. Soon, another ambulance arrived. Jasmine and Chance were hurriedly attended too and taken to each ambulance.

The police came over to Marlene and Zoya. "Were you the one who called 911?"

Marlene shook her phone at the officer. "I called."

"Did you see what happened?"

"We were driving and there were two vehicles a good bit ahead of us. One car moved to the right lane and the vehicle behind it moved to the right lane as well, then all we saw was the first car catch air and go down the hill."

"We will have to shut down this road to investigate what happened. Get back to your car and head home. Can I have your contact information just in case we have more questions?"

"Of course." Marlene offered up her contact information and Zoya's as well. They were too stunned to do much else but get home. Marlene helped Zoya get up the hill and as soon as they could they were told to do a U-turn and get home another way. "So that was Jasmine and Chance, right?"

"Yes. Oh my goodness."

"Maybe we should go to the hospital."

"No, we are not family, and they won't let us see them. They are going to the ER. Leonard is on call tonight, and they already called him in an hour ago. I can ask him what's going on."

Marlene parked the car in front of Zoya's house, and they both went inside to join their daughters in the sleep over. Zoya grabbed two glasses and filled them with water. The girls were still up being crazy and there was no need to disturb them. The girls knew they had made it home.

Zoya sent a text to her husband and she and Marlene went to watch TV. An hour had passed and the girls must have gone to sleep, it was too quiet. Zoya picked up her buzzing phone, it was Leonard. "Babe, Jasmine and her son Chance were in an accident."

Leonard took a few shallow breaths. "You two made it home and are safe, right?"

"Yes, we have been here a while now. Marlene is the one who called 911. We witnessed their car go into the lake."

"You two can't swim, did you go into the lake?"

"No, other people did. How are they?"

"Chance didn't make it. Look, I got to go. His mother is in critical condition, they are reading alcohol in her system. I will keep you posted. This is not good. The police have so many questions."

"Wait, Chance didn't make it. You mean he's dead…dead, dead?"

"Yes, he is gone, and his mother doesn't even know this yet. The police contacted his dad."

Zoya started to cry, tears streaming down her face, then she could hear a man screaming in the background and she knew that was Chance's dad hearing the news.

Leonard gathered himself. "I got to go. The father is here, I have to speak to him. I was attending to his wife. Dr. Brown was attending to his son. Like I said, it's not good. Bye. Love you."

Zoya looked at Marlene, now both of them were crying hysterically. They stayed up all night in disbelief.

Chapter 33

SOPHIE AND AALIA BARELY touched their breakfast after hearing the news about Chance and his mother. Granted they didn't like him, but they still felt bad about what happened. Aalia scraped at her pancakes as she started to formulate all the questions she had stewing in her head.

Zoya slurped down a bowl of cereal while Marlene poured a couple glasses of orange juice and quickly added a little vodka to both glasses. "Girls, are you doing okay?"

Aalia grunted an uh-huh before taking a bite of her cold pancakes. Syrup drizzled down her chin. She took the back of her hand to wipe the golden droplets away. "Okay, let's get the details straight. You two were driving back home and saw two vehicles. You said one changed lanes then the car behind it followed them to the same lane. Did you hear the cars hit? Like, did the other car hit them or did they just swerve off the road on their own?"

Zoya drank her juice in two gulps. She coughed lightly as the vodka taste hit the back of her throat. "Really, I don't know if the other car made contact with their car. I Just saw their car go down the embankment and the other car kept going, matter of fact I don't think their brake lights came on so they never slowed down."

"I really wasn't paying attention to those details. Once the car went down the embankment, I was really in shock and pulled the car over to help. Not that I was going in that water. I didn't realize the car had rolled into the lake until we got to the water's edge. The car went down fast too, right, Zoya?"

"Yes, it was like out of a movie. I just saw the headlights get dimmer and dimmer as it was sinking. Oh, can you imagine being trapped in a car that is filling with water?" Zoya shivered uncontrollably for a minute. She kept getting the chills since she heard Chance's dad screaming."

Aalia got up from her seat to go stand by her mother. "All right, so do you know who was driving?"

"It was Chance. I was there when Jasmine called her husband, and he sent Chance to pick her up. She even turned to me and said they live just up the street."

"So she couldn't drive?"

"No, she had a bit much to drink. Really, there were a lot of folks who drank too much. Not me or your mother, we paced ourselves."

"That rum punch was delicious." Marlene offered with a slight smile.

"You two really sound like alcoholics." Aalia pointed at her mother's empty glass. "Maybe when they pull the car out of the lake, they will know if the other vehicle hit it?"

"The officer said they had to do an investigation." Zoya turned to the front door watching Leonard walk in, he looked tired and hangry. She grabbed her plate, rushing up to him, offering him her breakfast. She quickly grabbed his backpack as he took the plate. He nodded at everyone as he kicked off his sneakers. He ate quickly and you could see his energy slightly pick up.

Aalia couldn't resist, she had to make her quick inquiries. "Is Mrs. Jasmine alright? Did the police talk to her?"

Leonard handed the empty plate to Aalia. "I am going to take a shower and get some sleep, but she is not doing well. She is awake and aware of what has happened, and she is grieving."

Everyone watched Leonard head off to get a quick shower in. It was one thing to treat strangers but to treat someone that your kids knew and they died. No parent can witness a child die or see the anguish that death causes another parent without feeling their pain on some level.

Chapter 34

••••

JASMINE SAT AT HOME alone and in a dark room. The curtains closed tight, to block out the sun and life outside while she bore the burden of death inside. She cried until she had no tears to shed, she stopped eating and didn't want to talk to anyone. She barely spoke to Craig. Together they were silent, apart they were silent. Since coming home, she sat in Chance's room without moving. Turning to glance at Craig, she felt her nerves start to fray under his presence. "What?"

"Do you remember getting hit, there was damage to the back of the car. The police are holding the car for now. I retrieved what I could. The insurance company is sending someone to look at the car too, but I say they cut the car as a loss. The police are still doing their investigation so they may question you again."

"You are saying we got hit? I remember Chance complaining, but I don't know what he was complaining about. I drank a bit, and I was so sleepy. I don't remember much. I hit my head, I felt water, I looked at Chance. My baby is gone, damn it. I should have died down there with him." Jasmine closed her eyes, wishing for tears but she had none to give. She turned back to her original focal point.

"We have to make arrangements."

"You do it!"

"I can't do this alone, he is your son too. You will regret not helping."

"I regret that I am still breathing and he is not."

"This is not healthy. I have had to look at my car knowing my son died in it. I got a call at close to midnight saying there was an accident. I rush to the hospital to you totally out of it and not only did I have to hear my son was gone, I had to go verify it was him. So don't sit here in some god damn realm of pity and act like you are the only one in pain. Get up, take a shower, and get in the car to get our son's body out of that god damn hospital. Eat something too."

"If I had just driven home, Chance would be alive right now."

"From the sounds of it, if you drove home, I would be making arrangements for you. Don't blame yourself. Maybe I should have picked you up, hell, I was home by that time. Chance was up and said it was just around the corner. He said he would be right back but he didn't come back!" Craig covered his face as he slid down the door frame. He could hear Jasmine shuffling across the room towards him. His tears drenched her shoulder as her body shook next to his.

Chapter 35

• • • •

BRENT SR. CARRIED A box full of Chance's belongings up to Jasmine. She stood stoically at the door, her face puffy, eyes sunken, and a few pounds lighter. She waved him in, patting him on the shoulder as he put the box on the bench by the door. He spun back around to gather the bouquet of flowers he had for her from his car. "This is my first time over to your house. Under the circumstances, how are you doing?"

Jasmine took the flowers and added them to the other arrangements she had received. "As best as I can. We are making the final arrangements. My parents are flying in today from Florida. I am not having a public service. The school wants to hold a memorial, but I will not be in attendance. You are more than welcome to attend and his friends will attend. That's it. No more, no less."

Brent Sr. offered a painful grimace. "Nobody can understand your pain and grief. I am so sorry this happened. If there is anything I can do just let me know."

"You have done so much already. Thank you for getting his belongings. It is all I have now. I tried so hard to protect him, to advocate for him, and to lose him like this. I blame myself. I should have just taken you up on your offer to drop me off. I am driving myself crazy with the options I should have chosen that night."

"This is out of your control. It was an accident."

"Was it an accident? Craig says there was damage to the back of the car. Someone hit us. I remember Chance complaining, but I was so drowsy. I hope we can track down any information about the vehicle that hit us, that person killed my son. I need justice for my Chance."

"We'll see what the investigation pulls up if anything. Send me the details. I will definitely be there."

"Thank you so much, Brent. You are always right where I need you."

Brent Sr. hurried back to his car, he had left his son in there and they were going to grab lunch and hang out. As soon as he got in the car, he gave his son a smile and shook him by the shoulder. "This is a hard time for them. You want to go with me to his funeral?"

"He is the last person I want to see even if he is dead. Jerk! Is it wrong that I am glad he is gone?"

"No, he was an asshole to you."

Brent Jr. picked at his thumb nail. "I'll go. Say good riddance. It's my last chance...get it? Last Chance. He was such a bitch."

"Language! I'll let it pass. Hold up did you say Last Chance? Damn, you are right, I guess this was his last chance." They laughed hysterically on and off for most of the ride. Brent Sr. looked at his son as they sat at a stop light. At least he didn't have to deal with Chance anymore. He felt bad for Jasmine but he had no good words or feelings for her son.

• • • •

NOEMI PICKED UP HER wine-stained dress from the cleaners. They did their best but she had let the stain sit too long. She was going to try her hand at it but if that didn't work, the dress was a loss. She sat on the bench waiting for Juan to come pick her up. Her stomach churned as she watched a car pass by with one of the school's magnets on the bumper. Not only was Chance dead, but now she was being charged with abuse and harassment, the school was still conducting their investigation and now the school was being sued by Chance's parents for not doing anything about their complaints. Noemi's teaching career was all but over. She could feel the school scrutinizing everything she had done, questioning their response or lack of response to Jasmine's complaints. Her termination letter was practically signed now that the school was listed in the lawsuit as well. She had to fight these false allegations but she could see the uphill battle looming, the cost, and cracks in the façade were getting harder to dismiss.

Noemi got up as soon as she saw Juan's car, she quickly got into the passenger side, increasing the air on her side. "This is a nightmare. Look at my dress. I don't even know who bumped into me. That night was a blur to be honest. I should not have gone. Why did I go? Mr. Walker reprimanded me too. I should have just stayed my ass home."

"I wasn't sure why you wanted to attend. I just assumed you were trying to let everyone see that you were doing great recovery wise."

"Yeah, if you say so." Noemi knew she would cause a stir. That is why she went. She knew Jasmine would be there, but maybe now that was not such a smart move. Her hand balled up into a fist. She sniffed softly, feeling her nose press against her bandage. At least the splint was off her face. What a difference three weeks could make. They got back home and she hurried out the car, passing from the garage to the steps. She tossed the dress on the couch then went to sit on the deck. She could sense Juan walking up behind her. He placed his phone on the table. She got this irritated feeling, she couldn't have her back to the deck door. She turned in her chair looking for someone, anyone. She got up uneasy, dragged the chair to the other side of the table so she could see the deck door.

Juan looked at Noemi, every hair on her arms was up. "What's wrong?"

"Nothing, I just can't have my back to the door."

"Never used to bother you before."

"Weird, huh?" Noemi listened to the birds' chirp and sing their little songs to each other. She felt uncomfortable. She got up to stand by the deck railing and instantly felt dizzy and threw up. She grabbed the rail as she lurched forward to expel every bit of food she had eaten. She could feel blood rushing out her nostril. She covered her nose as Juan rushed toward her with a towel. He pressed it against her face, wiping blood and vomit away. Noemi gestured towards the door, and they walked into the house quickly. She went to the bathroom to get herself cleaned up, her nose still bleeding profusely.

Chapter 36

• • • •

AALIA SHIFTED UNEASILY in her seat as the other classes clamored into the gym. The memorial for Chance was dragging on and many students were restless. Brent Jr. and a few of his friends snickered with their heads lowered. There were quite a few people who were not feeling sorry for the loss of Chance. He really rubbed a few people the wrong way. Aalia stared at a few of Chance's classmates, then at Mr. Walker who was giving a rousing speech, talking very positively about the one student who was always in his office. Mr. Walker stepped off the stage to let some other teachers offer their condolences. It wasn't like Chance's parents were there so who was this directed to? Many people were very glad he was gone even if it was through death. You never wished death on someone, but an exception could be made for Chance.

Aalia rose from her seat, fortunately, she was sitting at the end of the row. She nodded at her teacher as she went to stand outside the bathroom. Some parents had come to the memorial, they stood in the back looking solemn. She saw a few people cry, but they were caught up in the shock of it. She decided to get a sip of water then just sit on one of the benches outside. She was over the service. Everyone started to file out of the gym and head back to their classes. Aalia waited patiently to see her classmates then entered the fold as they returned to the main building. She looked at Sophie, who looked pale and sickly. "Are you okay?"

"Cramps. I don't think I can make it the rest of the day. Will you be okay?"

"I will be fine. I have some pain killers, if you want?"

"You know we can't take medicine like that...but palm me two when we get to class."

Aalia pushed her way through a pack of seniors so she could get to the classroom and her backpack before the teacher. She quickly rummaged through one of her backpack pockets and got the Tylenol ready to hand off to Sophie.

Sophie quickly walked over to Aalia, grabbing the pills and taking a few hard swallows of her water. "I am so struggling right now. Oh, you missed it; Brent Jr. and a few of his friends had a huge chuckle while one of the teachers was talking. Mr. Walker gave them a death stare."

"There were a lot of people who were not sad. Not that I expected folks to be, but he died. A little decorum, right?"

"Don't worry about it. Everyone reacts differently to death."

"These folks are in their real feels."

"And there is nothing you can do about that. Don't stress out."

Chapter 37

• • • •

ZOYA PARKED BEHIND Marlene in the pick-up line, with an hour to pass before the kids were released. Her bangles clinked and clanged against each other as she opened her door to go sit at one of the picnic tables under the trees. She waved at Marlene as she hurried over to join her. She plopped her water bottle down on the table as she swung a leg over the bench.

Marlene tapped the table with her knuckles as she stared Zoya down. "The funeral is this Saturday but only family and close friends. His classmates are going."

"That's going to be a tough one for Jasmine. I feel awful for her. I can't even imagine what she's going through."

"I know, right?! Just awful." Marlene watched Brent Sr. hop out of his car to go get his son. "Looks like Brent got a new car."

Zoya turned to look at the vehicle. "Doesn't he have a huge truck?"

"He has the truck and a fancy car. You know he has the fancy car for when he is in realtor mode. So this car is new or his wife's car. I don't know him like that."

Zoya turned back to face Marlene. "Oh yeah, he was the realtor for the Jimenez house."

Marlene tapped the table, her memory kicking in to what she wanted to discuss with Zoya. "Get this, I was driving by Lake Whetstone and the tire marks are still on the road. There was definitely a car behind Jasmine and Chase, and the tire marks of the car behind them appear to be from larger tires. I'm no detective, but I think they were not just hit but intentionally run off the road. You can see where the larger tire tracks followed them."

"So you think the investigators of the accident will come to your same conclusion?"

"I think so. I kind of want to call the police officer who gave us his information and see if I can tell him what I saw."

Zoya scrunched up her lips, thinking back to the accident. "So you think the vehicle was a truck? I swear everything happened so fast. I think it was a truck...like one of those really jacked up trucks. I was kind of tipsy so my memory is foggy. Do you have any other information to offer the police?"

Marlene watched Brent and his son exit the school and head to the car. "I don't think I have anything new to tell them but one of the moms here, her husband is an officer...maybe he heard something. You have seen the dad a few times."

"Duh, he comes here in his patrol car. He might be here now. We got time...want to walk down the line?"

Marlene didn't need to wait for Zoya to finish her sentence as she was already up and walking down the line of cars. They walked quickly and saw the police car off in the parking lot. Marlene looked at Zoya, both of them beaming from excitement. They crossed the street, climbed up the embankment and stepped into the parking lot. They quickly waved at the dad as he lowered his window. Marlene looked at him, giving him a short and quick smile. "Hi, I'm Marlene and this is Zoya. Our daughters are a couple grades behind the senior class. We witnessed the accident with Chance and his mother. I was wondering if we could ask if you heard anything about the investigation? I think they were run off the road. We saw it happen and we think a truck ran them off the road."

"Hello, I'm Brad, my kid is in the 11th grade. I haven't heard much about the accident. Believe me, when I heard who it involved, I went and did some inquiries. I know they are investigating the scene. The mother doesn't remember much so any information you all as witnesses can provide will be helpful. Officer Tony Santiago may be working this case I can give you his information so you can touch base."

Zoya crossed her arms, uneasiness sweeping over her. "So this is now a criminal case?"

Brad shook his head not trying to divulge too much. "Off the record, I think this is in limbo but could be leaning towards charges if we can track down the other vehicle involved. Definitely talk to Tony."

Marlene and Zoya waved at Brad then hurried back to their cars. The kids would be dismissed soon and they had to decide on if they were going to have a talk with Tony.

Chapter 38

••••

ZOYA SAT QUIETLY ON her deck, enjoying some grapes. She passed the time as best as she could, but her anxiety was steadily increasing. Marlene had sparked a strong desire to piece together everything that had happened by Lake Whetstone. Suddenly, she felt three soft taps on her shoulder and turned to see Aalia looking at her. "Can I help you? You need a snack?"

Aalia shook her head as she pointed to the kitchen. "Marlene is here and she brought Jasmine."

Zoya shot out of her chair totally in shock. "Marlene did what now? Jasmine...here?" Zoya hurried into the house to greet her guests. She looked down at her outfit to make sure she looked decent. Not even a text message from Marlene. Who just shows up to a house with Jasmine in tow? "Hi, ladies."

Zoya, unsure of what to do, opened her arms, embracing Jasmine into a secure hug. She could feel her body sink in as she cried on her shoulder.

Jasmine released her grip on Zoya. "I'm so sorry but I ran into Marlene and she told me that you two may have some information to offer the police. I have talked with them, but I really have no recollection of much. Marlene mentioned the skid marks she saw which backs up Craig's idea that we were hit. I was really out of it, but I remember Chance complaining about the driver behind us. I hit my head on the dashboard and then I just remembered being in the water."

Marlene pointed at the couch. "We believe a bigger vehicle was behind you. We think it was a truck. I didn't get the plates, but as your car went over the embankment I know the truck kept driving. No brake lights or anything."

"Maybe they were drunk" Zoya added. "I mean I was tipsy."

"A drunk driver. Could it have been one of the parents from the school? It could've been anyone." Marlene looked at Zoya, desperate for an answer.

Jasmine gripped her purse, her mind was racing. "What if it was intentional? I need to talk to Brent. That stupid wench, Jimenez was at the fundraiser. For what? She had no business on that campus. I raised this point with my attorney."

Zoya shook her head, disagreeing with the thought that Noemi had anything to do with the incident. "You can't believe she was involved."

"Why was she there? She wasn't supposed to be on campus so why show up then? She knew I would be there, but she didn't think my Chance would be picking me up?" Jasmine stood up and started pacing back and forth.

"Didn't she leave early?" Zoya fiddled with the bead bracelet on her wrist.

"She should not have been there at all."

"It couldn't be her."

Jasmine bit her bottom lip. She fished her phone out of her purse. "I didn't think about it until now, but that woman had so much motive. I will give the police a call right now. Thank you both. I will keep in touch."

Zoya stood in her living room in shock. It was well known that Noemi and Jasmine did not get along. There was actual hatred that fueled Jasmine. Could Noemi really be that vengeful? Chance had his fair share of people who didn't like him, but nobody knew he would be in the car that night. Frustrated, Zoya threw her hands in the air. "I need a drink!"

Chapter 39

••••

MARLENE POURED HERSELF a third glass of wine. She was getting dizzy, watching Zoya pace around the deck. "So what had happened was, I went to the grocery store and I ran into Jasmine. So we are talking, right, and I tell her our observations and she kind of perked up in her rage fueled ways. The investigation apparently shows that another vehicle hit her car. They are looking into finding the vehicle. They are looking at paint they found on the car and checking with any body shops to see what vehicles have come in that could potentially match up with the damage done to the car."

"That is fine, but Jasmine is now going after Noemi and getting the police involved."

"I see where she would think that. By all rights, Noemi should not have been there and she could've just waited for Jasmine to leave."

"Does Noemi have a damaged vehicle? I know we are stuck on a truck, but I don't think she has a truck."

"Maybe Juan has a truck."

"We don't know if it was a definite truck...okay, I believe it was a truck."

Marlene put her glass down. "We can't even assume that the culprit is someone Jasmine knows. It could have been a random drunk driver."

Zoya looked at her glass of wine. "Remember all the confusion at the fundraiser. Someone spilled wine on Noemi. Noemi left the fundraiser."

"But remember Mr. Walker had already run into Jasmine and told her he would ask Noemi to leave."

"Oh yeah, you are right. All right, so Noemi leaves and let's say she's hanging out in the parking lot. She really stayed out there that long to see when Jasmine would leave?"

"I just don't see it, but I don't think Noemi is that type of person."

"You know Noemi had her moments. You heard some stories while you would be in the office. I'm not saying she's a murderer but the accident turned deadly. It wasn't planned."

"If someone was targeting Jasmine it could be planned."

"Noemi wouldn't do that."

LAST CHANCE

Marlene washed out the empty wine bottle then placed it in the recycling bin. "Let's just see how things play out. Maybe while we are at the school, we can look to see what other people from the fundraiser saw or heard. I guess we need to talk to Tony."

"Let's wait on talking to Tony. Let's see how things go with Jasmine looping in Noemi."

Marlene gave Zoya one of her reassuring hugs. They rocked side to side before releasing each other. "Something tells me this was not an accident."

Chapter 40

• • • •

NOEMI INSTANTLY REGRETTED going to the fundraiser now that the police interrogated her, questioned why she was at the school, where she was after leaving the school, and took photos of her vehicles. She already was under investigation for abuse and inappropriate interaction with a minor. Jasmine escalated those charges, and she was now in a legal battle. All of her interactions with Jasmine and Chase were now like targets on her back. Even Jasmine being arrested for assaulting her in the parking lot was now being used against her and she was the victim.

Noemi rubbed her temple as a migraine was trying to make an appearance. She never got migraines, but since her accident, they were now a consistent companion. She grabbed a tissue, wiping her nose. A deep crimson blot of blood stained the tissue, her head now pounding, she got up to get some medication that she knew wasn't going to even phase her. She grabbed her car keys and phone. She was going to try and get to the emergency room. The drive that normally took ten minutes was dragging on. Her peripheral vision was decreasing, she glided through the intersection unaware of the light being red. Her car ran into another car coming to an abrupt stop. She rested her head on the steering wheel, then she felt her door open and instantly felt several punches to the side of her head. She quickly raised her arms to block the assault then she heard the high pitch shrill of Jasmine's voice.

Jasmine landed blow after blow then grabbed Noemi, dragging her out of the car, laying her out on the street. Jasmine landed one swift kick before some man grabbed her and pulled her away from Noemi. Jasmine looked up at the man recognizing him. "Dr. Leonard Thompson?"

Leonard watched the police arrive with an ambulance. "Are you okay?" He could see the panic in her eyes and realized she may be having some flashbacks to the accident. He motioned for one of the EMT's that he recognized. "Sam, get her to the ER. I will be there shortly." He rushed over to Noemi and motioned for the police. "She ran the light and hit that lady. I'm an ER doctor, I will go with her to the hospital."

Chapter 41

Jasmine woke up in a panic, she clawed at the air as she sat up. She looked around the room realizing she was in the ER. "Where is she, that bitch hit me." She swung her legs over the side of the bed, pulled the curtain back and stared up at Craig, his face devoid of color.

Craig put his arms up, trying to keep Jasmine where she was. Tears streamed down his face as he gently pushed her legs back up on the bed. This was the same space Chance was in when he had arrived at the hospital. Resting his hands on his knees, he cried hysterically, waving a hand at a nurse approaching to calm him down. "I can't be here in this place right now."

Leonard told the nurse to take Craig out as he evaluated Jasmine. Post Traumatic Stress was emanating from Jasmine and Craig. "I spoke with the police. I told them that the other lady ran the red light and hit you. You are going to get an MRI done. You hit your head and that collar bone needs to be looked at. You may have a fracture."

Jasmine reached for her head feeling the lump then she reached for her shoulder, wincing in pain. She laid her head on her pillow just as some techs came to whisk her away for her X-rays.

• • • •

NOEMI LOOKED AT JUAN, her migraine was releasing its strangle hold on her. She spoke with the police and got cited for reckless driving and a few more charges. At this point, she was collecting charges left and right.

Juan shook his head disappointed in Noemi's decision making. "What were you thinking? Where were you going?"

"I was coming here. My migraine was terrible."

"So, call me or call the ambulance. You blew through a red light. You could have killed her. You weren't wearing a seat belt. You are lucky."

"A red light?"

"Of all the people to hit you had to run into her. She's suing the hell out of us...now this?"

"Who did I hit?"

"You hit Jasmine. Oh Lord, she is going to bankrupt us." Juan paced around the hospital room, his patience wearing thin. "Until they decipher what is going on with you, no more driving. Not like I'm letting you use our only available car any time soon."

"That's why I was coming here, these migraines are getting worse and my nose bleeds. I wanted them to scan my head or something." Noemi watched Juan pace around the room. "I may have had some vision issues while I was driving."

Noemi reached for her face, the swelling was definitely tender to her touch. She drifted off to sleep. She was barely aware of what was going on and had no energy to try and make sense of the mayhem she created.

Chapter 42

••••

ZOYA DREW IN HER ROBE as Leonard retold the story of Jasmine and Noemi. He was very animated even though he had a grueling work schedule. Zoya leaned against the tall dresser, her mouth twisted in a smirk. "You witnessed the accident and Jasmine recognized you. Wait, you said she dragged Noemi out of her car?"

"That was the crazy part. The accident happened and I saw Jasmine get out of her car. I think she recognized Noemi, and she just ran up to the car, opened the door and went off. Really, Noemi is a mess. She was kind of zoned out even when Jasmine was on her. I honestly think Jasmine was in a PTSD fit."

"That's bonkers. So Noemi was having a medical emergency and flew through a red light. She can't catch a break."

Leonard munched on some chips. "The police were having a long conversation with the Noemi lady. You said Jasmine thinks Noemi is the one that hit them?"

"Yes, it has gotten rather messy. I don't think Noemi did it, but she does have a lot of pock marks on her. I can see where there would be a motive."

"Hmmm, interesting. Well my name is Bennett and I'm not in it. I must say it was so hard to see Jasmine's husband back and having to relive the loss of his son. The same triage room he came to find his son. Ugh…it was rough knowing he knew exactly where he was."

"They haven't even had the funeral yet. It is all too much." Zoya took off her robe, tossing it on the chair. She had a lot to tell Marlene in the morning.

••••

MARLENE WRUNG HER HANDS as she listened to Zoya, then threw up her hand to stop Zoya mid-sentence. "Wait, wait, let me hop in. I talked to another parent that was at the fundraiser. Amy said that Mr. Walker was having a heated discussion with Noemi after the spilled wine incident. She also said that she observed Noemi's car was still in the parking lot even after she was told she had to leave. Now, how long she was there, we don't know. Also remember that Mr. Walker came back to talk to Jasmine and reassure her that Noemi was gone then he went about his business."

Zoya paused, her finger resting on her chin as she shook her head. "Okay, I see you and I raise this observation. Aalia came home and told me that at the memorial she saw many students being disrespectful. The boy Chance harassed was laughing. The teachers were pretty decent, but she saw some teachers kind of over the memorial."

"Sophie had mentioned that as well, but I really thought that this is a really emotional incident, and many people don't react the same way. Also, I can see where people who had issues with Chance aren't going to be shedding any tears over him."

"I see your observation, and may I add that Amy said that she overheard Brent Sr. curse out Chance in the hall. She said she was around the corner and saw Brent run up on Chance, and Chance backed away in fear then ran off to class."

"Whoa, what?"

"Yes, this is what I am trying to tell you. Brent Sr. went all the way off on Chance."

"So Chance never reported that to anyone. Maybe Jasmine has no idea that this occurred. She and Brent work in the same circles, they are always hanging out."

"If Chance knew the Brents why would he harass Brent Jr.?"

"What if they didn't know each other? Just because Jasmine knows Brent doesn't mean Brent knew Chance. See it this way, Chance and Brent Jr. don't know each other's parents. If my child was having an issue with Aalia but I know you are Aalia's mom, wouldn't I talk to you about what was going on? So why didn't Brent Sr. talk to Jasmine about what Chance was doing?"

"Brent Sr. didn't know Chance was her son. Wow!"

"We still can't assume this though. We need proof."

"Did we just add Brent and Mr. Walker to a short suspect list?"

"We added them right up there with Noemi. Mr. Walker has had to go back and forth with Noemi over Chance. There is bad blood between him and Jasmine. Jasmine has come at Mr. Walker consistently."

"I think we need to gather some more information. We can touch base with Jasmine. Something tells me Officer Tony will be contacting us." Zoya and

Marlene gave each other a high five then left to get a walk in before stopping to get a salad. Things were starting to get more interesting.

Chapter 43

• • • •

NOEMI LOOKED AT THEIR bills, knowing Juan had to pull the lions share since she was not getting paid. She pushed the grocery store paper to the side, her eyes seeing a letter with the school's emblem on it. Her heart skipped a beat, she took in a deep breath and opened the letter. Two pages listing every complaint and issue leveled against her with the final paragraph informing her that she was terminated from her teaching position. She dropped the letter on top of the stack of medical bills and invoices for all the services she received. She looked up at Juan as he entered the kitchen, the look on her face speaking volumes. "I am officially terminated." She clenched her jaw as a migraine crept in, her temple throbbing and the pain increasing sharply with every second. "I need to lay down, pass me my prescription."

Noemi took her medicine and went to the couch to recover. Juan brought a cold damp cloth, handing it to Noemi so she could place it on her forehead. "We have savings, but these bills and the new mortgage are going to drag us down. We need to hunker down."

Noemi slept her migraine off, then woke up still groggy but remembering her reality. She sat up rubbing what remaining sleep she had from her eyes. She shook her head apprehensive of what her next moves would be. She reached for her phone, based on the text messages that had come through, some of her former coworkers knew she was no longer affiliated with the school. She steadied herself before rising from the couch. The room was dimly lit but she could smell dinner being made. She slowly walked to the kitchen, overhearing Juan engaged in a tense conversation. She rounded the corner, she caught him finishing the call. "What's up?"

"She's suing us and our insurance. Fuck!"

"Who?"

"You ran into Jasmine, remember? I told you she would ruin us."

"I wish I never met that woman or her son."

"You should not have driven that day. We are going to be hemorrhaging money. Oh my! I need to make a drink. You ran a red light, went into an intersection, and hit the worst person. I need to think."

Noemi picked up the court letter from the counter, her name in bold caught her eye even before who the letter was from. She ripped the envelope open then dropped her head in annoyance. "I have to appear in court for the accident. I guess in all the drama the police wrote me several tickets." She neatly refolded the letter, then placed it under a heavy-duty magnet on the fridge. She grabbed a pen so she could put her court date on the calendar. "I am not hungry." She left the kitchen to go to her room and wallow in self-pity. She was annoyed at herself but still had more than enough room to lay some blame on Jasmine and her nuisance of a son, Chance. "I am so glad that idiot is dead."

Chapter 44

••••

CRAIG AND JASMINE STOOD together while looking down at Chance. Jasmine cried uncontrollably as she was directed back to her pew. The service went on for an hour, but Jasmine lost track of time. It was as if she was outside of her body, staring at everything around her. Her body was as close to lifeless as it could get. She looked up at Brent Sr. and some of the other classmates who were invited to attend. She nodded at Marlene and Zoya appreciative of their coming to support her.

Marlene and Zoya got in Zoya's car and made their way to the procession. They drove past Lake Whetstone on their way to the cemetery. "It was nice of some of his classmates to come."

"It was so sad. Jasmine is being strong about it, but I know her heart is broken."

"We aren't supposed to bury our children."

Zoya parked the car and opened the doors. "You ready?"

Marlene put on another coat of lip gloss before following Zoya to the gravesite. They stood with some of the parents, most of whom they didn't know. Marlene could feel her nose running, she sniffed hard as tears filled her eyes. She grabbed Zoya's arm for support then turned around to go sit on a nearby bench. She saw Zoya's headlights flash, realizing Zoya had unlocked the doors for her. She quickly made her way to the car and sat there watching the priest say his last words. Marlene pulled down the visor to look at herself. She let out a gasp as she noticed one of the cars had some damage in the front. She spun her torso around so she could get a better look. It was one of those beefed-up trucks. She grabbed her phone to take a picture. She examined the picture, seeing a woman standing a bit away from the truck. She turned back around and could see the woman was watching their group. She squinted her eyes. "Is that Noemi?" As soon as she said the name out loud, the woman turned and walked off just as a police car was driving past.

Marlene quickly hustled herself out of the car, jogging to catch up to the woman. She was glad she opted for flats instead of the cute wedges. Scurrying across grass and between the graves, she arrived just in time to see Noemi get into a car. Still holding her phone she recorded the moment as Juan and Noemi drove off. She exhaled loudly. "Gotcha!"

Marlene ran back to the car as guests were returning to their cars. She ran up to Zoya out of breath. She got into the car quickly buckling her seat belt. "Noemi was here watching the service, and I see a truck here with some damage to the front. You think we should tell Jasmine?"

"Not now, she just buried her kid."

"Yeah, you're right. I am getting caught up in the moment." Marlene punched the air several times. "Why would she show up to this? Someone is looking like a primary suspect."

"Okay, pot stirrer. She could have been here to visit someone and just so happened to see this funeral."

"Stop it! Throw caution to the wind and create drama with me."

"We will be at the restaurant soon. Let's get some food and formulate a plan."

"I didn't see who the owner of the truck was."

"What if that truck wasn't part of the guest list? It could just be some other person's truck."

"I got the plates and details in a picture. I also have a recording of Noemi and her husband."

"Busy bee I see."

"You know I keep my ear to the ground and eyes on the prize."

Chapter 45

• • • •

MARLENE AND ZOYA PLANTED themselves at one of the tables, watching the other attendees arrive and making small talk with people at their table. Zoya turned to Brent Sr and his son, observing as much as she could. She glanced at Marlene taking a sip of her soda, then turned back to Brent Sr. "So, do you still stay in contact with the Jimenez family?"

Brent grabbed a piece of bread from the breadbasket. "Not so much, now that the deal has been completed. I will stop by just to make sure everything is alright. Too late for buyer's remorse." He chuckled mostly to himself.

"Marlene saw them at the cemetery."

"What? They were there…why?"

"We don't know why. We didn't want to say anything to Jasmine. Didn't want to start an issue if there isn't one."

"True, but it seems weird for them to be there under the circumstances."

"Exactly. Marlene said by the time she got close enough, they were driving off. She couldn't decipher if they were there for personal reasons."

"Not like the funeral details were a secret. Any of the teachers could have given her the details. But they all knew it was a private service. Jasmine only let people she wanted to be around her to attend. Only his closest friends were allowed to attend."

Marlene nudged Zoya, agreeing with the Jimenez crew being at the cemetery as being totally suspicious. "Just seems weird. Was she there to be nosy or out of spite?"

"Why would you say that?" Brent leaned towards Zoya and Marlene, making sure the other table guests weren't involved in their conversation.

Marlene lowered her voice. "Looks like the accident wasn't an accident. The police may be pressing charges, and they are looking at potential suspects."

Brent's eyes opened wide with shock an intrigue. "Oh wow! Now Noemi looks really suspicious. Damn. Have the police tracked down the vehicle?"

"They are still working on that, and Zoya and I will relay anything we remember to the police."

"Wait, you were there?"

"We were driving behind the truck and saw her car go into the lake."

Brent scratched his chin as he leaned back in his chair. He looked at his son and his friends cutting up next to him, quickly giving them a stern stare. He shook his head and shifted his posture before making contact with Jasmine. After a brief nod in her direction, he turned back to Zoya and Marlene. "I had offered to take her home that night."

"When you were outside with her, did you see Noemi?"

"I wasn't paying much attention, but didn't she leave after the wine incident? I thought Mr. Walker was going to ask her to leave?"

"Apparently, she didn't leave straight away."

"Many people were tipsy from the fundraiser; it could have been a fellow parent, or just as easily a random person."

"I don't think anyone from the school has had any issue with Jasmine."

"You sure about that?"

Brent started to think about what he was hearing but he couldn't believe anyone would be so upset with Jasmine to cause her any harm. He tossed his napkin on his plate. A sense of uneasiness came over him.

Chapter 46

••••

"THAT BITCH! ARE YOU serious right now? She had the nerve to be at my child's funeral." Jasmine sprang up from her couch, enraged with the gall and audacity that was Noemi Jimenez. "Why was she there? I need to inform the police." She paced around her living room with her hands shaking. She snatched her keys off the coffee table, and made her way to her car. "I am coming over there, Brent."

Brent tried to diffuse the situation. He needed to reason with her. "What, where? To my house?"

"No, I am going to Mrs. Jimenez to ask her why she was at my son's funeral. She is a predator. She was harassing my son while she was a teacher and has the nerve to come to his funeral."

"Wait, listen, don't do it. Tell the police. Is there a case where they are investigating her?"

"I filed charges, yes. Also, the school is still doing their investigation. I am suing the school and her."

"All right, then you don't need to be caught at her house. Then you look bad. Tell the police."

"Who saw her there?"

"Zoya and Marlene told me they saw her. They didn't want to tell you because they didn't want to upset you."

Jasmine dropped her keys into her purse, looking at her feet still in slippers. She turned back to the living room. "Let me give them a call." Jasmine looked up at Craig as he entered the room, her eyes lowered to look at her phone. "She was there at our son's funeral."

"Who?" Craig grabbed the blanket off the back of a chair and tossed it at Jasmine.

"Noemi Jimenez."

"No, she wasn't."

"Yes, she was watching us at the gravesite. Zoya and Marlene saw her."

"Oh, really? I wonder if the police officer who was in attendance saw her."

"Oh my goodness, that is right. We had an officer there. I need to talk to Zoya and Marlene." Jasmine got hold of Marlene and Zoya on a group call. She fixed her hair, rubbed her tired eyes, and let out a slow breath. "Hi, ladies. How are you doing?"

"We are good. We are actually together at my house." Zoya positioned her phone so she and Marlene would appear on one screen. "How are you doing?"

"I am doing as well as a person who just buried their only child can do. Anyway, I heard that you all saw Mrs. Jimenez yesterday."

Zoya looked at Marlene than back at Jasmine. "Marlene saw her, but we decided not to say anything out of respect for your son and the situation."

"I totally appreciate that. I know now and I am going to let the police know that she was there. Actually, we had an officer there. He was monitoring the funeral to see if anyone out of place would show up, and I say Mrs. Jimenez is that person."

"Really? Is this for the school investigation?" Zoya grimaced a bit, lost for words.

"It was in part for that. You may not know this but we are suing the school and Mrs. Jimenez. The school did nothing where my complaints were concerned and then for Chance to admit that Mrs. Jimenez was doing way more than he let on. Now my child is gone and the police are looking for the other driver."

Marlene waved her hand. "I saw a truck at the cemetery that had a lot of front-end damage. I think the truck belonged to someone who was attending the funeral. I was going to give the make and plates to the police."

"I really appreciate that. I just hope that vehicle wasn't involved in my accident. I can't imagine someone we know running us off the road. But I can see Mrs. Jimenez being a total ass and doing that."

"We don't think Mrs. Jimenez left the school when Mr. Walker asked her to leave."

"Yes, Brent mentioned that. I will tell the police about that, too. It's time for them to look as closely as possible at Mrs. Jimenez and determine if she had anything to do with my car being run off the road and the death of my child."

Chapter 47

••••

MARLENE SLURPED HER soup, burning her tongue in the process. She grabbed her bread and dumped it in the broth. After her conversation with Jasmine she was very eager to find out why Mrs. Jimenez was at the cemetery. Could it really be a coincidence? No way. Of all the cemeteries to be at, and just happen to be near where Chance was being laid to rest? The thought sent a shiver down Marlene's spine. Marlene glanced across the table at Sophie who was busy texting Aalia while munching on her ham and Swiss sandwich.

Once her bread was fully saturated with soup, Marlene resumed eating. She wondered how Jasmine's conversation with the police went. "Sophie, slow down, you are eating too fast."

Sophie stopped mid-chew to point at the door. "Mrs. Jimenez."

Marlene's eyes grew wide as she turned to look at the disgraced teacher. "Oh my goodness. I need to talk to her."

"Mom! Really?"

"I'm just going to say hi and ask a few questions."

"Don't offer up anything."

"Look at you, all knowledgeable. I got this." Marlene waved at Mrs. Jimenez and gave her a warm smile. She watched her glide between tables. "How are you doing?"

Naomi dabbed at her nose with a tissue. "I'm doing okay. Still recovering. How are you two doing?"

"Good, have a seat with us after you order your food." Marlene patted the table while grinning. Her eyes darted from side to side with glee.

Sophie shook her head just about over her mother's antics. "Real smooth."

"I know, right!" Marlene finished her soup as Noemi returned to the table. She gave Noemi a quick look. "I was wondering what you thought of the Casino Night."

Noemi laughed, her eyes cold and distant. "It was very nice to see everyone. I was very pleased with the turnout. My dress was ruined, but what can you do...right?"

"Why did you attend? I mean, you know, it was so soon..."

Noemi's gaze grew focused on Marlene. "That is a good question. I kind of was on a selfish kick. I was out of the hospital and wanted to see people. You know, like let everyone see that I was recovering."

"You knew Mrs. Wright would be there."

"I didn't go to see her, but I knew she would be there. That's a shame what happened to them that night."

"Her son died, that night, that's heartbreaking."

"It's a tragedy." Noemi got up quickly to retrieve her food. She placed her tray on the table and started to eat.

"Did Mr. Walker ask you to leave?"

"Yes, I was a distraction. After my dress got ruined, I just went to the bathroom to kind of clean up."

"Yeah, makes sense." Marlene crossed her arms across her chest, her brows scrunched together. "I could have sworn I saw you at Chance's funeral...at the cemetery." She glanced at Sophie then back at Noemi.

"I was at the cemetery but not for Chance. I was visiting a friend. Died of cancer, she did." Noemi lowered her gaze suddenly. "I got fired from Holy Trinity. This investigation and lawsuit is taking its toll on me. I should go. I try to get out but it's just a lot. My career..." Tears streamed down her sunken cheeks. "It was nice to see you both. Have a great year, Sophie. I miss you and Aalia."

"Oh, don't be upset. I know you are going through a lot."

Noemi shrugged her shoulders. "Even in death, Chance is working my nerves." Noemi wiped away any last remaining tear. "Not me speaking ill of the dead."

Chapter 48

• • • •

BRENT STOOD IN HIS driveway inspecting the shutters as Juan gave a detailed summary of issues. He listened momentarily baffled by the size of the nest by the window. Why would a bird build a nest there? He shook his head then turned towards Juan. "Why were you at the cemetery? Of course that looks suspicious."

Juan paused to look at the nest. "Jasmine had police at the funeral. So now my wife is being questioned. Like, was that a crime?"

"Why were you there? What did you tell the police?"

"I told them the truth. Noemi went to visit a friend."

"Of all the days to visit, you guys went the day of Chance's funeral? This friend died recently?"

"I don't know the lady. Noemi can't get around like she used to. She came to me and said she needed to go see her friend. I honestly didn't know the funeral was that day or even at that cemetery."

"Well, did you talk to the police together?"

Juan shook his head. "No. Oh no. I never asked Noemi what she told the police." Juan started to panic, suddenly aware of the optics.

"I don't know what to tell you. Your wife is under investigation, they are watching her."

"Noemi didn't do anything wrong. We just went to the cemetery. Why was there police at this boy's funeral?"

"I think the investigation about the crash is turning more criminal than an accident. I mean it was an accident, but the person fled. That's a crime in itself."

"Noemi didn't run them off the road, she came home, the car was fine. Her dress was ruined."

"Why did she even attend the fundraiser?"

"I told her not to go, but she insisted. She wanted to see her friends."

"Or she wanted to be seen."

"What does that mean?" Juan shot back.

"She knew Jasmine would be there. Why antagonize her like that? She was suspended and she was not allowed on the campus. Why go to the fundraiser?"

Juan walked to his car, irritated by the direction the conversation had taken. "I got to go."

Brent waved then turned to look at the nest. He reached for his phone to give Jasmine a call. There was a lot for them to discuss. "Jasmine, you wouldn't believe who was here?"

Jasmine honked her horn as she pulled up to Brent's driveway. "Say it to my face."

Brent's jaw dropped as he ran up to Jasmine's car. "What?"

Jasmine got out of the car quickly and gave Brent a hug. "Who was here?"

"Juan. I asked him point blank why was his wife at the funeral. He mentioned the police questioning them. He was very concerned with their stories not being straight."

Jasmine clenched her jaw tight. She could feel her teeth grinding against each other. "If that woman had anything to do with my son dying…"

"Did the police say anything?"

"I haven't heard anything, but I knew they were going to question them."

"What about the vehicle that hit you."

"The police are looking at the street cameras. This is an active investigation. Mrs. Jimenez has a motive. She was at the fundraiser, and she apparently didn't leave the fundraiser until after I left. She was there the whole time."

"Are you serious? We were there for a good two hours after she was asked to leave."

"The police got surveillance footage from the school. It shows her leaving the ladies room and then going to the parking lot. She sat in her car. She was in the parking lot. She didn't leave until after I left. Nobody was checking to see if she actually left the campus."

Brent felt a lump in his throat, his mouth went dry. "This isn't looking so good."

"The police checked both of their vehicles. No damage, but that doesn't rule her out. They're watching her."

Chapter 49

MR. WALKER LEANED AGAINST his desk, arms crossed and deep in thought. He listened to the detective go over the security footage they had reviewed. He shook his head wary of the path Mrs. Jimenez was taking. "I can't say for sure that this person is Chance. You are saying that's his backpack?"

The detective replayed the loop showing the suspect approach a car, pull out some cylinder and deface the car. "Yes, we showed this to some of the faculty and a few teachers mentioned the backpack as belonging to Chance. We also have footage of him leaving the gymnasium and heading in the direction of the teacher's parking lot, then he returns to the gym."

Mr. Walker dropped his arms to his side. "Have you mentioned this to Mrs. Jimenez or the boy's parents?"

"Yes, based on this information Mrs. Jimenez is going after Mr. and Mrs. Wright for damages."

"Oh, why is she going after them? They have already lost a child. They don't need this."

"Mr. Walker, would you say that Mrs. Wright was liked by everyone? Did Chance get along with everyone?"

"Listen, Mrs. Wright and her son were complicated. Both of them found an issue with so many things and people. Mrs. Wright is a complaining person. Nothing was ever right where her son was concerned."

"Was Chance a bully? He has plenty of complaints from parents, students and staff."

Mr. Walker strolled back to his seat, grabbing a file dedicated to Chance. "Mrs. Wright never took responsibility for her son's behavior. He would start a fight and she would swoop in and defend him. He was at fault more times than she would like to admit. There were several complaints about him. There were a couple of boys he really picked on. Brent McGregor and another boy. Really those boys hung out but I have met with the McGregor kid and his dad. I believe they may have pressed charges over the cafeteria incident."

The detective jotted down his notes, taking names and requesting a copy of Chance's file. "Would you say there was a hostile relationship between Mrs. Jimenez and Mrs. Wright?"

"I can't say hostile, but they did not like each other. I believe Mrs. Jimenez had a confrontation with Mrs. Wright not just on campus but off campus too. I recall her telling me she called the police and Mrs. Wright was arrested. I myself had to have Mrs. Wright banned from the campus. I witnessed her assault Mrs. Jimenez in her classroom. Her entitled and rude behavior was getting out of hand."

"How was your relationship with Mrs. Wright and Chance?"

"Cordial, but I'm not going to lie. I dreaded seeing her strutting up the walkway. From the time I saw her, I knew it was going to be a disagreement. You just can't win with her. She will fight tooth and nail for her son. Then the investigation into Mrs. Jimenez and her interactions with Chance, let's say that just made things that much more insane."

"If I have any more questions I'll be in touch. Oh, one more thing. Mrs. Jimenez hasn't been cleared of the allegations Chance made, right?"

"No, that investigation is still ongoing." Mr. Walker watched the detective leave. He exhaled as he wiped the sweat from his brow with one hand and loosened his tie with the other. There was a lot more going on than the detective was going to actually divulge. Mr. Walker picked up his phone to call the school's attorney. He needed to fill them in on his conversation with the detective.

Chapter 50

••••

BRENT SR. LEANED BACK in his chair, watching a man walk up his driveway. He didn't recognize him and assumed he was a solicitor. He watched his son run up the driveway to the front door. "What's up, son?"

"Dad, there's this police guy here to ask us questions."

"Say what?" Brent strolled past his son, making his way to the door. He opened the door, concern quickly spread across his face. "Can I help you?"

"Mr. McGregor?"

"Yes."

"Hi, my name is Tony Santiago. I'm a detective with the Piedmont Police Department. I wanted to see if you and your son had time to answer some questions regarding Chance Wright."

Brent's heart literally skipped a beat or two. "Sure, come in." He stammered as he backed away to let the detective in.

"Thank you." Detective Santiago quickly scanned the room then walked into the living room to take a seat. "I gathered information from Holy Trinity, and I saw many complaints against Chance Wright. I also saw that your son has had a few incidents with him. Was Chance picking on you?"

Brent Jr, stood next to his dad. "Every day he harassed me. I never did anything to him. I even asked him one time why he was messing with me."

"Did you ever see him bothering any other students or teachers?"

"Yes, he picked on a few students. He even bothered some teachers but that was just his attitude. He got in plenty of fights with me and other students."

"Can you name the teachers he bothered with his attitude?"

"Mrs. Jimenez, Mr. Walker, and Mrs. Roberts."

"Mr. Walker, the principal?"

"Yes. Chance and Mr. Walker would go back and forth. He had a few suspensions."

"Mr. Walker had to deal with Chance and his mother a lot, it would seem."

"Yes. I kind of felt bad for Mr. Walker. Mrs. Wright would just go off."

Detective Santiago continued to take his notes. He gestured at Brent Sr. "Do you know Mrs. Wright?"

Brent shook his head. "Yes, she's a realtor at another office. We ran into each other a lot so we became friends."

"Did you know her son?"

"No."

"But you are friends?"

"Really, I never met her son. Even though our kids go to school together, I never met him."

"Your son had several run ins with him, and you still never met him?"

"Mr. Walker never met with all of us at the same time. Me and my son would meet with Mr. Walker and Chance and Jasmine would meet with him separately, so I never saw him, nor did I ever connect him to her. In all honesty we would just talk about Chance. I never knew who his mother was."

""When did you find out Chance was Mrs. Wright's son?"

"Actually, I met him at a house showing and that was it."

"Seems like Mrs. Wright had some contentious interactions with several teachers and Mr. Walker. Did you witness any issues?"

Brent scratched his head. "Can't say that I did. I heard about it."

"Who would you hear this from?"

"From my son and other parents. You would not believe the gossip you can get while in the carpool pick-up line."

Chapter 51

••••

"DID YOU EVER SEE OR hear of any altercations between Chance or his mother with students or staff?" Detective Santiago cracked his knuckles unconsciously before picking up his tablet.

Zoya looked sheepishly at Marlene then at their daughters. "Really, there was always some drama. We would hear about incidents from the girls and of course other parents talk. You know gossip."

Marlene shook her head in agreement. "Jasmine spent a lot of time in Mr. Walker's office due to Chance picking on his classmates. He really honed in on the McGregor boy, and of course, there were several issues with Mrs. Jimenez."

"You both have witnessed incidents while in school?" Detective Santiago turned to look at Aalia and Sophie. The girls appeared very animated and intrigued by the questions.

Aalia clasped her hands over her chest with glee. "Chance instigated several fights with Brent and some of his friends. He never got along with Mrs. Jimenez. He was disrespectful, disruptive and annoying. There was always an argument between them. Mrs. Jimenez just stopped responding and would ignore him, but she was still trying to be a good teacher."

"Chance was always being sent to Mr. Walker's office. There have been a few times when people overheard them yelling at each other. Of course Mr. Walker got everything under control, but then, Chance's mom would show up, and she was a nuisance too." Sophie chimed in with her sing-song voice. "Do you think there's something ominous going on?"

Detective Santiago chuckled, his cheeks turning red instantly. "Oh, no, just trying to get some information."

"Is this part of the investigation that got Mrs. Jimenez removed from the school?"

"In part, yes. Speaking of that, did you all witness any inappropriate behavior between Mrs. Jimenez and Chance?"

"Can't say that I did." Aalia's gaze dropped to her lap.

Sophie waved her hand frantically. "I never saw anything but Mrs. Jimenez kept Chance behind a lot."

Aalia shot Sophie a glare. "That could be because she wanted to talk to him about his behavior."

"You just told the detective that Mrs. Jimenez stopped responding to Chance. So why keep him after class? Mrs. Jimenez had shut down for months. Practically everyday, Chance was working her nerves."

"That's not fair, Sophie."

"We weren't there, but the detective asked if we saw anything and that's what I saw." Sophie returned her gaze toward the detective. "Other students have mentioned what they saw to Mr. Walker. The truth will come out. I'm not bashing Mrs. Jimenez, I'm just looking back now and trying to see if there were red flags that I just dismissed."

Detective Santiago shook his head as he took down notes. "Listen, you are doing the right thing. You can only speak to what you saw and sometimes you have to go with your instincts. You are not bashing anyone."

"So what about Mrs. Wright putting hands on Mrs. Jimenez and Mr. Walker?" Aalia spat the words out, annoyed with the whole line of communication.

Detective Santiago looked puzzled "Mr. Walker never said anything about Mrs. Wright touching or hitting him."

Marlene scrunched up her face, visibly upset about the incident. "Jasmine got in Mr. Walker's face a few times. One time, she poked at him, on his chest."

"You witnessed this?"

"Unfortunately. I was returning the key to the uniform room, and you could hear those two going at it. I walked in and saw her invade his personal space and she poked him. You know, like this." She got up and shoved her fingers onto Zoya's shoulder several times. "Mr. Walker backed up and smacked her hand. It was intense. It wasn't much later that he banned her from being on the campus. She was literally in his office every week because of her son."

"I will speak to Mr. Walker again. Thank you for this. I didn't realize it had gotten so bad. Mrs. Wright was not a nice person and her son was not too far behind her."

"You are trying to see if they had any enemies?" Zoya smirked unapologetically.

"It would seem the Wrights were spreading more vinegar than sugar."

Chapter 52

• • • •

JASMINE SAT AT THE light two, cars behind Noemi, having followed her for a few minutes. She casually drove past her and parked a few spaces away. Watched Noemi enter the store. Jasmine got out the pocketknife from her purse, gripping it as she scurried toward Noemi's vehicle. She pretended to need to tie her shoe then stabbed at the back tire several times. The last strike punctured the sidewall. The hiss of air was slow and steady.

Jasmine got to her feet and quickly made her way to the store, grabbing a cart and browsing the aisles. She quickly spotted Noemi and sped up her pace, ramming her cart into the back of Noemi's legs. "Oops!" She pulled the cart back then rammed it back into Noemi.

Noemi crumpled to the floor, looking up at Jasmine.

"You molested my son! You sick bastard!"

Noemi looked at the other patrons in horror, her voice barely a whisper. "I!"

"And you had the nerve to show up at his funeral." Jasmine shrieked. "I will make you pay."

Noemi looked helplessly at the crowd, sprang to her feet fully embarrassed and ran out of the store. She got in her car, backing out of her space as quickly as possible then sped off. A loud popping sound got her attention then the car leaned to the left as she was taking the turn rather quickly. She panicked as she slammed on her breaks, sending her into a spin. She hit her head on the steering wheel as shattered glass fell around her. Her body slumped on the roof of the car. She shook her head, realizing her car had flipped over. She felt hands pulling at her retrieving her from the car, sunlight hit her face as she stared at the devastation around her. Another car was damaged sitting on the side of the road, her car was upside down, and people were pointing in her direction. She promptly passed out, her body limp against the Good Samaritans side.

Noemi's eyes fluttered open, and she blinked at the brightness. She brought her hand up to her forehead, recoiling when she felt the knot on her head. She tapped her forehead a few times then looked around at her surroundings. She was in the hospital. Again. She felt the brace on her leg as she tried to lift it.

Juan approached the bed agitated. "Honey, are you okay? I don't think you should drive anymore. You caused so much drama today. Another accident. This time the car is totaled. You hit two other vehicles."

Noemi shook her head in shock. "I was in an accident?"

"The police want to talk to you. Our insurance is going to drop us. Oh my goodness, we are going to get sued by how many people?" Juan spun around as a nurse entered the room.

"I don't remember what happened. I don't remember an accident. I saw Jasmine."

"She is going to be out and about. You have bigger issues than her now."

"She cornered me in the grocery store. She was spewing lies and causing a scene."

Juan raised his hand to silence Noemi. "Jasmine has nothing to do with you causing a huge accident and crash." Juan swiveled his head upon hearing the door open again. This time, the nurse came in with a police officer. Juan instantly got a headache. Here we go, he thought to himself.

Chapter 53

• • • •

JASMINE STARED AT DETECTIVE Santiago, her cup of coffee raised to her mouth. She could feel doubt entering her mind. She just let a little air out of Noemi's tire, she didn't expect a whole blow out. "So, how bad is she?"

Detective Santiago glanced at his notes. "It was bad, car flipped, hit two other cars, several people were injured and are in the hospital."

"So, how can I help you?"

"I just have a few questions. There are a few incidents where your son had altercations with other students and you had a few altercations with teachers and Mr. Walker. It was determined that your son spray painted Mrs. Jimenez car. What was the issue the two of you were having?"

"My son was having issues with Mrs. Jimenez in particular. She was using her authority to hold my son back and hamper his education. She alienated him and after allegations of inappropriate behavior came up, it just made more sense. Because my son was trying to avoid her, she did everything in her power to sabotage him."

"When you ran into Mrs. Jimenez at the grocery store, you confronted her…did you know about the allegations at that time?"

"I am not sure."

"When you were at the school fundraiser, did you have any interaction with Mrs. Jimenez?"

"No, but she should not have been there. She was not supposed to be on campus due to the investigation about her conduct."

"You said that Mrs. Jimenez was antagonizing you."

"Listen, I was defending my son. All my interactions at that school was in defense of my son. We brought up all the issues with Mr. Walker and nothing was done. They are liable for so much. Why was she at the fundraiser? When she was told to leave, she didn't, and we ended up getting run off the road. She left, soon after I left."

"You believe she had something to do with your incident?"

"Yes."

"Have you ever thought that you and your son ruffled feathers?"

Jasmine blinked totally unaware of what Detective Santiago was suggesting. She thought about her run ins with a few people. "You think I made an enemy?"

"Maybe a few." Detective Santiago looked at the list of names to jog his memory. "You were confrontational with Mr. Walker and Mrs. Jimenez, and this was witnessed on several occasions by several people, your son has a whole file for fighting, picking on, bullying, being argumentative, suspensions…the list goes on. I have spoken with a few people and you two were not high on the list for most likable."

Jasmine's heart sank as she became aware of how her approach may be seen as annoying and negative. She was just trying to be an advocate for her son. "So, you think maybe someone from the school was out to hurt me and my son?"

"The investigation has determined that your car was more than likely hit intentionally and by a vehicle that was considerably higher than your vehicle. Witnesses mentioned a truck exact make and model not known. Camera footage does show your car at the intersection and then there was a truck going above the speed limit going through after you…maybe four minutes behind you. There's no cameras after that intersection for two miles and plenty of places for that truck to have turned off."

Jasmine felt her fingers go numb and quickly sat down as Craig opened the front door, standing there and watching everyone.

Chapter 54

• • • •

DETECTIVE SANTIAGO sat across from Juan as Noemi answered questions on the phone with her insurance company. He offered a twisted smile as he tried not to eavesdrop. Looks like some of the victims have lawyered up and the insurance company was already backing out as much as they could. Typical response for a big company. Another glance at his watch and he could see Juan pacing around the small room.

Noemi ended her call, her heart pounding at the revelations set before her. She racked up several tickets and court dates. This was her second accident. All of these cases were going to bankrupt them. She swallowed hard before raising her gaze back to the detective. "Every time I think this situation can't get worse, it actually does."

Tony smiled as it was all the comfort he could offer. "I'm sorry to bother you, I had a few questions. You had several run ins with Mrs. Wright and her son. Would you say they were well liked?"

"They were annoying, moreso Jasmine. Oh, I ran into Jasmine at the grocery store and she bumped into me with her cart. Then she started yelling at me and accusing me of harming her son. It was so overwhelming, I just ran."

"Did she hit you with her cart on purpose?"

"I really don't know, she was behind me, I wouldn't have even noticed her if I didn't get bumped. Listen, we shop in the same shopping centers, I'm not going to stop my life on the notion that I may run into her. Now, she could've hit me on purpose, but I can't one hundred percent say that."

"This is the second time she has confronted you in that shopping center. Back to my question, enemies, you think anyone at the school would want to harm them?"

Noemi scrunched up her nose, fighting a sneeze. "They had more people that disliked them than I could count. You can't treat people the way they do and expect to be liked. Now outright hurting them, yes, I could see it, but not what happened to Chance. You know, maybe a bad thought. People can wish harm to a person."

"Did you wish harm on them...hypothetically speaking, of course."

"I'm not going to lie, I wished Jasmine off a short pier several times. She's just grating my nerves and she's rude, obnoxious, and spiteful. As much as she says I was lording my authority over her son, she's the one who is always threatening people and the school. I was so relieved when Mr. Walker banned her from the campus. She's a terror."

Detective Santiago scratched his chin, seeing a clear pattern of Jasmine's behavior. "I'm seeing that. Seems like a lot of people may have been too scared to say much and if nothing was being done to curb their behavior…why would anyone say anything?"

"Exactly, it was more whispering behind backs. What's the point of speaking up if leadership won't hear or listen to you. It's only when Mr. Walker started to really get the brunt of her wrath that he even really started to do something. If he hadn't walked in and witnessed her coming at me, who knows. I probably would've never brought it up."

"The investigation showed that the vehicle that most likely ran the Wright's off the road was a truck, you know the big ones. There was footage of one following their car that night. You all don't own any trucks, do you? Do you know if any staff members have one?"

"I never really paid much attention. Maybe. The parents have trucks and jeeps. I have seen them at the carpool. Now that's just what vehicles I can see. I have had to go to my car and carpool parents start lining up a whole hour before school ends. There's quite a line too."

"Even if we include the parents, who picks the kids up could be a grandparent, so the vehicle may not be the regular pick-up car. I don't think the school keeps track of parents' cars or even records them."

"There's cameras outside of the school, they may pick up the cars as they go through carpool. They monitor the front of the school."

Detective Santiago needed to see any video of the carpool. Maybe the truck belonged to a parent. He still needed to know what the staff drove too. He had a gut feeling that the Wrights struck a raw nerve and someone from Holy Trinity had had enough.

Chapter 55

••••

MARLENE AND ZOYA STARED at the screen, scrutinizing every pixel. They watched as the Wright's car passed through the intersection, followed a few seconds later by a large truck. Marlene pointed at the screen. "Zoom in. Can you all do that?"

"We can't really do that. The quality of the footage is really determined by the camera being used to record everything." Detective Santiago smirked, knowing real life detective work wasn't as fancy as how it's shown on TV or the movies.

"Well, that's definitely the truck that was in front of us. It's not the clearest image, but I distinctly remember a truck and then saw Jasmine's car swerve off the embankment."

"Do you recall being behind this truck the whole time?"

Zoya looked at Marlene briefly, her memory shifting to that horrible night. "The truck was speeding. Remember, you made the comment that the vehicle behind you was coming up on us quick, then the truck switched lanes, passed us and was gone."

Marlene remembered how annoyed she was when the headlights came up behind her blinding her. "Yup, you are right. This truck came from behind, then when we caught up we saw the accident. We didn't even really catch up, we just got there in time to see the accident and then stopped to help. We didn't even know it was Jasmine and Chance in the car."

Detective Santiago wrote all of this new information down. He could see Zoya's mind working. "Have anything to add?"

Zoya pointed at the screen with the truck frozen in time. "There's no plates or they are covered so you can't read them."

"Covering plates is illegal. We are trying to determine that information. Again, the footage isn't the best."

Chapter 56

• • • •

JASMINE AND CRAIG STOOD over Chance's grave, adding flowers where the headstone would be. Jasmine's grief still raw dragged her down to her knees, the wail that escaped her mouth was loud and sharp. Her face now inches from the ground, she pounded the earth with her fist. Craig stood by her knowing she was inconsolable. He turned to the sound of a vehicle coming to a stop and parking. He turned to watch the door open and out sprang Detective Santiago. He didn't even notice them he was on a mission and headed over to another section across the street. Craig watched him look at his phone and stop in front of a tree then back to his phone. He was trying to place himself...find something.

Craig tapped Jasmine then headed off in Detective Santiago's direction. His steps turned into a jog then a minor sprint. "Detective Santiago?"

Detective Santiago looked up from his phone, squinting then getting his bearing. He continued to look at the headstones and plaques around him. He took several photos. "Mr. Wright, how are you?"

Craig stopped short of breath. "Could be better. How are you? Visiting someone?"

"No, I don't know anyone here. I'm following up on Mrs. Jimenez's friend." He formed air quotes around the word friend. "I asked her why she was here that day, and she said she was visiting a friend. Based on what a witness said, they placed her around here. Mr. Jimenez doesn't know who this friend is, and Mrs. Jimenez never provided a name. My gut tells me she wasn't here to see anyone but you all. I will be talking with her again. It's all my opinion right now. Let's say it's a hunch."

Craig turned to look at his wife still crumpled on top of their son's grave. "I will leave you to your work. If that woman had anything to do with this?" Craig pointed at his wife, his heart sinking further into their shared grief. "No parent should bury their child." Craig's voice cracked as he turned around to walk back to Jasmine.

Detective Santiago looked back at the plaques, continuing to take pictures. He got what he wanted and hurried to his car. He had to get to the hospital and question Mrs. Jimenez.

• • • •

BRENT SR. GRABBED A box from his trunk. He was helping Juan move some things into the garage. He was shocked to get a call from him but was willing and able to help a client out. "Juan, what is going on? What's all of this stuff?"

Still flustered by the nearly daily reports from his insurance company, Juan glanced at his phone. Detective Santiago was at the hospital talking with Noemi and he realized he wouldn't be able to get there. "Listen, this whole accident is getting out of hand. We are being sued by the insurance companies and the victims. I've hired an attorney. We are bleeding money already and we haven't even gone to court yet. Noemi is no longer working, it's my income alone and I don't know if I can keep us afloat." Juan grabbed the box out of Brent's arms, placing it in the back of the garage. "We may have to downsize. I can't believe this…we just got this house, but if things don't shake, I can't afford this."

Brent went back to his car to get more stuff and hand it off to Juan. "Listen, don't say that. Everything will work out. If you want, I can meet with you to talk about your options."

"I really appreciate that. I'll be right back, let me grab you a water."

Brent ran to his car to grab one last bag and quickly stacked it on a box. He left the garage and stood in the driveway as Juan came back out with a water. "Thanks. I'm going to head out. I have a house showing to get ready for."

Chapter 57

• • • •

DETECTIVE SANTIAGO dabbed at the side of his mouth as he stared Mrs. Jimenez down. "So, the name of your friend you were visiting is?"

Noemi stared at him blankly. "What?"

"Your friend who died, what's her name?"

"What does that have to do with anything?"

"Why can't you answer?" Detective Santiago stood in his superman pose getting annoyed with Noemi.

Noemi shook her head. "I don't see..."

"That's okay, you are being released from here so we can meet at my office. Maybe then you will see a formal reason to answer my questions."

Noemi's heart skipped more than two beats. The detective was being serious enough to bring her in for questioning. "Detective, I can't remember."

Detective Santiago lowered his gaze. "You can't remember your friend's name?" He winked as he turned to leave, and he stopped a few steps before the door. "I'll have a patrol car swing by and pick you up, you get released around 2 today. See you later."

Noemi panicked as she rushed out of her bed. "Wait, I just am under a lot of stress, my memory gets foggy. There's no friend. Oh God, please."

"Why were you there?"

"I got the details from a coworker and I just wanted to pay my respects."

"Pay your respects for a child you had issues with, a child that alleged misconduct on your part? Really? Or maybe you just wanted to see the misery you caused."

Noemi grabbed at Detective Santiago's arm, desperate to get her point across. "It wasn't like that. I was wrong. I shouldn't have gone. I just was not in my right frame of mind I wouldn't want to hurt anyone."

Detective Santiago removed his arm from Noemi's grip. "Which coworker gave you these details?"

Chapter 58

••••

ZOYA STACKED BOOKS on the shelf, she was volunteering at the school's library while Marlene was organizing uniforms for the used uniform sale. Just a few more books to be put in their proper place and she would be done. She waved at the librarian then headed over to the storage room.

She tucked a few strands of her spiraled hair behind her ear as she leisurely strolled down the hall. She could hear kids clapping in one classroom and a teacher trying to regain control in another classroom. A smile spread across her face as she remembered her days as a student. Zoya finally made it to the storage room and could hear Marlene huffing and puffing. She heard a familiar voice and curiosity took control, dragging her past the storage room just a bit further. She saw the police officer, she forgot his name but he was a parent to one of the students. He was having a conversation with Detective Santiago. Oh wow, why was the detective here? Play it cool. Zoya didn't want to appear as nosey as she actually was. She should turn around and go to where she should be. The thought crossed her mind, but curiosity again was in control. She found herself walking right up to the men. "Hi."

Detective Santiago nodded and gave her a quick handshake but he didn't let go of her hand. "That tip your friend told me was good."

"Marlene? Which tip?"

"Mrs. Jimenez was not at the cemetery to visit a friend. She was there to watch the boy's funeral. If you remember anything don't hesitate to tell me. I will follow up on all leads." Detective Santiago looked at his watch then at the front office. Mr. Walker opened the door ushering the detective in. "Well, I have to meet with the principal."

Zoya waved at Mr. Walker then said goodbye to the officer and quickly made her exit. She ran to the storage room to find Marlene struggling under the weight of a bin of boys' khaki pants. She grabbed one side and together they rested the bin on the table. "Girl, Detective Santiago is here, and he said your tip was a legit lead."

Marlene dropped her elbow on the bin. "Say what now? Tell me!" She pointed at the door, letting Zoya know she should close it.

Zoya closed the door and ran back to Marlene. "Noemi was at the cemetery to watch Chance being buried.

Marlene snapped her fingers knowing Noemi looked suspicious. "That's messed all the way up. She would've gotten away with being seen if I didn't see her."

"The detective is talking with Walker. I wonder why?" Zoya separated pants by size as her mind kept churning with questions. "Oh, I was in the library and the library lady said Noemi was released from the hospital. She is going through it. I had Leonard check in on her covertly. They are being sued left and right. Mr. Jimenez is beyond stressed out."

"Well, that's a lot. I wonder if they have any more leads on the truck?"

"Maybe that's why the detective is here, to look at the vehicles. You really think it was one of the school's employees or parents that did this?"

"I don't know who, but I'm sticking with our suspects list." Marlene packed up the separated pants and moved onto a bin full of girls' skirts and shorts. Marlene shifted her weight to her other leg as she saw a pair of pants that didn't make it to the now organized bin. She grabbed the pants, held it up them looked at the tag to see what size it was. She felt paper crinkle in one of the pockets and reached in to retrieve it. She unfolded the paper and let out an audible screeching noise. She shoved the note at Zoya as she looked to see who the pants formerly belonged too. The carpool number was 180 and the last name was Wright. These were Chance's pants.

Zoya grabbed Marlene and marched out of the storage room up to the front office just in time to see Detective Santiago opening the door. "Detective."

Detective Santiago closed the door then approached Zoya. "What's wrong?" He could tell that something was amiss.

Zoya handed him the note. "This was in these pants, the pants were Chance's."

Detective Santiago looked at the note, his eyes widened then narrowed. "Meet me after school. We need to talk. Signed Mrs. J." Tony folded the note and placed it in a zip lock bag. "I stay prepared to collect evidence. Can I have those pants too?"

Zoya obediently handed over the pants then Zoya looked at Marlene nodding at her. They were on a roll.

Detective Santiago smiled broadly. "You two have been very helpful. Remember, tell me anything you remember or think of."

Chapter 59

••••

BRENT SR. LEANED AGAINST his car, waiting for Jasmine to arrive. He was helping her with a listing. Honestly, he wasn't sure she should be alone, and he definitely was shocked she wanted to even work right now. Maybe work would keep her mind busy and less stuck in grief. He looked at his phone. Jasmine was on her way. Brent looked up as a car pulled up there was no way potential buyers were showing up already. He waited. His jaw dropped when he saw Detective Santiago. How does this guy find him? "Detective, hi."

Detective Santiago made his way over to Brent. "Hey, sorry to bother you. I was talking to Mrs. Wright, and she said you would be here. Can I ask you a few questions?"

"Of course, do you want to go inside, the owners aren't home."

"Sure. You were the Jimenez's realtor, right?"

Brent escorted Tony into the house, leading him to the living room. "Yes."

"They moved recently, and I was wondering why they left their previous home. It's just the two of them and their new house is considerably more expensive."

Brent scratched his chin, thinking back to the buying process. "Well, their current home was at the top of their purchasing ability. Actually, I just met with Juan and they are potentially looking to offload their home. He's the only one working and looks like they have a lot of legal issues. One thing after another."

"In your honest opinion, could they afford their home?"

"With both incomes it was still going to be tight. But they would've been fine."

"Did they have issues with money? Living above their means?"

"I can't say. Paper wise, they look good. Good enough to secure their mortgage. I don't delve too deep in financial stuff. Don't go making big purchases before signing the documents."

Detective Santiago looked at the entryway as Jasmine came in. "Mrs. Wright."

Jasmine wagged her finger at the detective. "Just Jasmine, please. I'm so happy to see you. You are working so diligently on this case. I brought coffee." She handed everyone their coffee then went off to the kitchen to set up.

Detective Santiago took a sip, the coffee warming his soul. He needed this boost too. "You are on the student financial board?"

"Yes but really, I just take notes at the meetings."

"Mr. Walker said you recently came to him questioning where some money had gone."

"Yes, I was going through some spreadsheets and noticed some money was not accounted for. I made Mr. Walker aware and he was going to let their accountant look into it."

"You only discussed this with the principal?"

"I mentioned it to the chairperson for the association just to keep him in the loop."

"Great. Thank you for your time."

Brent got up to walk the detective to the door. He stood at the doorway, observing a few cars parked in front of the house. "Jasmine, we got some folks here."

Chapter 60

••••

NOEMI TOSSED THE FOLDER on the table, it was full of court documents and the first wave of hefty fines and court fees. She checked her bank statements and she still hadn't received her last paycheck. She called the school and left several messages but nothing. Not one call back or email. The silent treatment was deafening. She couldn't even drive up there because she was without a car. They couldn't even look at replacing her car.

Her phone lit up. Finally, Doris from Human Resources was contacting her. "Hello, I've been trying to get in contact with payroll."

Doris didn't skip a beat. "About that, you won't be receiving your last check. Everything is on hold while this investigation goes on."

"What does the investigation have to do with my paycheck?"

"You were assisting with the student finance association and there's a discrepancy with the allocation of funds."

"You are accusing me of stealing money from the fund?"

"You will hear from accounting and the archdiocese has an open investigation. Have a blessed day."

Noemi sat there dumbfounded. "Have a blessed day." The words slithered out of her mouth just like Doris said it. The doorbell rang, shaking her free from her moment of shock. She listened as the bell chimed again. She got up, getting to the door. She paused, knowing the figure outside was Detective Santiago.

"Mrs. Jimenez, you didn't expect to see me so soon, huh?" Detective Santiago smiled.

Noemi backed away from the door. She was not in the mood, and she definitely didn't have the energy to deal with any more drama. "How can I help you?"

"I got some questions. You know the deal by now. Lovely place you have here. New development too."

Noemi nodded. "Thank you, I guess."

"How are you affording all of this?"

Noemi scoffed at the question. "Just fine."

"Are you having any money problems?"

"What? No!"

Detective Santiago looked around from the doorway. "Is there a reason why you were taking money from the student fund?"

Noemi's head started to pound, she was getting lightheaded. He already knew about the missing funds. She just found out about it a few minutes ago. Her hand landed on the door frame, barely holding her up. "I didn't take any money. I was assisting the accountant with spreadsheets. That was all I did. Look, I just got out of the hospital and I'm really still not fully up and running."

"No worries, Mrs. Jimenez. Rest up. I'll be back."

Noemi quickly shut the door, ran to the bathroom and threw up. Everything was coming at her too fast and she could never get proper footing. She was sinking with no lifeline in sight.

Chapter 61

• • • •

JASMINE CLUTCHED THE pants Detective Santiago had given her. That was really sweet of him to turn them over to her. She still wasn't sure why he had them, but she was overjoyed to receive it. This pair was from last year, she must've donated them back to the school over the summer since Chance outgrew them. She placed the pants on Chance's bed, his room just as he had left it. She closed the door determined to not cry. She went to her office to work on documents. She secured a buyer for the house Brent helped her with. Brent was so supportive, and she was grateful for his assistance. She knew he was concerned for her. She needed to work. To fill her days with tasks. She no longer had to work her schedule around Chance's schedule. She didn't have to get to the carpool pick-up line and sit there waiting for Chance to hop in the car. Chance took up so much of her time and thoughts. For him to be gone was a hole she could not fill.

Jasmine called Marlene. She smiled briefly, letting go of her desire to cry. "How are you, Marlene? Is Zoya with you?"

Marlene giggled. "Of course Zoya is here. I'll put you on speaker."

"Hey, girlies. I just needed to talk to some sane people." Tears streamed down her cheeks, her face hot to the touch. "Detective Santiago was just here, he's a sweetheart. He checked in on me and dropped off a pair of Chance's pants."

Marlene could hear the sadness in Jasmine's voice. "That was nice of him. He told you about the note?"

Jasmine felt a lump form in her throat. "What note?"

"The note I found in the pants. It was telling Chance to meet Mrs. Jimenez. As soon as we read the note Zoya took me, the pants and note to Detective Santiago. He was at the school meeting with Mr. Walker."

"Aha, he didn't mention that to me. Thank you for turning it over to him."

"No problem. Maybe it will be as helpful as Marlene's hunch." Zoya chimed in.

"What hunch was that again?" Jasmine increased the volume on her phone.

"Remember Marlene saw Mrs. Jimenez at the funeral? Well Noemi kept saying she was there to visit a friend, but Detective Santiago says he questioned her and that was just a cover. She was there to see the funeral."

Jasmine stared at the phone in disbelief and disgust. "I have some paperwork to draft up. Maybe we can grab lunch on the weekend." Jasmine ended the call without waiting for a response. If Mrs. Jimenez didn't get arrested soon, she was going to be found in a ditch. Jasmine was going to let the system work but she was willing to get her hands dirty. Mrs. Jimenez was going to pay one way or another.

Chapter 62

••••

ZOYA ROUNDED THE CORNER running into Brent. She backed up, waved, and laughed awkwardly. "Hey, how's it going?"

Brent placed his hand on Zoya's shoulder aware that he had startled her. "I'm good, and you?"

Zoya tapped at the folder in her hands. "Doing great. I'm here for the meeting...something is going on with the account."

Brent shook his head knowing all too well what was going on. "Yes. Looks like someone was skimming funds out of the account."

"No! Are you serious?"

"Yes. We are here today to answer some questions for the archdiocese and the school's accountant."

"Do they know who was taking the money?"

"I think they do. I noticed a discrepancy and told the chairperson. I think the school has tracked the person down and they just want to get our version of everything." Brent stared past Zoya and waved at another parent. He pointed at the door to show Zoya where the meeting was going to take place.

••••

MARLENE SAT ACROSS from Jasmine, polishing off her second glass of wine. Despite the circumstances, Jasmine appeared to be holding up reasonably well. Marlene listened as Jasmine unleashed a torrent of profanity and frustration aimed at Mrs. Jimenez. The woman really got under Jasmine's skin and had been testing her patience. It was clear; Jasmine absolutely hated Mrs. Jimenez.

Jasmine finished her third glass of wine. It was time for another bottle. She waved for the waiter to return to their table. "Can we have another bottle? Anyway, thank you, Marlene, for letting me vent. I just can't get over that woman. How dare she?"

Marlene watched the waiter open the new bottle of wine and place it on the table. She quickly poured wine into Jasmine's glass and the empty glass meant for Zoya. "I'm so sorry." Marlene looked at her phone seeing a text from Zoya letting her know she was at the restaurant. She waved at Zoya as soon as she saw her.

Zoya scooted into the booth next to Marlene. "Sorry I'm late. That association meeting was not a meeting."

Jasmine's eyes lit up with interest. "What happened?"

"Long story short, an employee was skimming money out of the association. The school's accountant and some investigators for the archdiocese questioned us."

Jasmine's lips puckered as if she tasted something bitter. "That heifer was stealing from the children. Reason ten thousand why I can't stand Mrs. Jimenez."

Zoya smirked. "How did you know it was her?"

"She worked with the accountant. Brent had mentioned noticing a discrepancy. None of us had any interaction with the money. She and the accountant handled any donations made on-line and cash donations were handled by her."

"Well, the accountant can be in on it?"

Jasmine shook her head vigorously. "It was Noemi. I can feel it in my bones. I even told Mr. Walker, but he dismissed everything, and I assumed he did nothing, but now it's a whole to do so he can kick rocks."

"An investigation is open. From what I got from the little inquisition, your guess is correct. Mrs. Jimenez is the one they are looking at."

"Bingo!" Jasmine tossed back her wine. "Let's order some pasta."

LAST CHANCE

Chapter 63

• • • •

NOEMI LOOKED AT HER bank statements seeing extra payments made to her account and a few paychecks were definitely higher than normal. She was good for not looking at her bank statements, she just knew money was there and never felt the need to look or dispute anything. She had spoken with the investigators and they showed every transaction. As much as she denied stealing from the association there was the evidence. What was she to do? She headed downstairs to retrieve a package that was dropped off. She opened the door and there was her package in the hands of Detective Santiago. She stepped back as she tried to calm herself down. "Yes?" She peered behind the towering detective, seeing several police cars with officers strolling up to her door. "Am I under arrest for the money?"

Detective Santiago handed Noemi the search warrant. "We are here to search your residence. Please have a seat with me in the living room."

Noemi observed the officers flooding through her house, practically upending every room. She saw one officer emerge with her laptop and a hard drive, while another officer came from the kitchen carrying bags, displaying their contents to a colleague. Anxiety began to creep in, threatening to spiral out of control. "Where are they going with my stuff...that's my husband's..."

Detective Santiago explained the search warrant and what the officers were doing but not what they were looking for. After a few hours Noemi had her house to herself. She watched the last police car leave, then stood in her home which was now a mess.

• • • •

DETECTIVE SANTIAGO sat in his car eating a sandwich. He had been parked up the street from the Jimenez home. He saw Brent drive up and leave after an hour. Not much going on, but there was something not right with Noemi and her connection to Chance.

He reviewed his notes and the alarming number of complaints Noemi, Chance, and Jasmine had against each other. The vitriol between Noemi and Jasmine was noticed by everyone.

Santiago picked up his phone, swallowing his last bite of his sandwich. "Detective Santiago."

"Hi, It's Brent McGregor."

"Hello, Mr. McGregor, what's up?" Detective Santiago brushed off some crumbs that fell on his shirt.

"Hey, I was by the Jimenez house and they are a bit rattled. They said you had a search warrant. Anyway, while I was there, I think I saw something out of place. They have a bunch of boxes, and I think one of the boxes had things that belonged to a student. They don't have any kids and it had the school's logo on it. It may be nothing, but it was just weird."

"Where did you see this box?"

"I was in their garage. Back wall, right corner, next to a ladder. I was there because they may have to downsize. I was kind of doing an appraisal for them just in case they want to pull the trigger and sell the house."

"They are looking to sell?"

"Well, only one income and they are burning through money."

"Thank you for the tip. I will look into it." Detective Santiago started his car and cruised right up to the house. He parked and ran up to the door. Juan answered the door. "Mr. Jimenez, may I come in?"

"Sure, excuse the mess, we're still trying to get back to normal after your guys came in here. What do you need now?"

"Can you show me your garage?"

Juan lead the detective to the garage. "Didn't your friends sweep through here already?"

"They did." Detective Santiago went to the boxes in the corner and could see the school colors. He grabbed the box, pulling out personal items of a student. He flipped the sweatpants over to look at the tag and saw a label with Chance's name on it. He showed the sweatpants to Juan. "Is there a reason why you have Chance's personal items?"

Juan looked confused. "No. I mean I have never seen those items."

"Where is your wife?"

"She's upstairs napping."

"All right. I'm taking this box with me. I'll be back."

Chapter 64

• • • •

NOEMI, STILL GROGGY from her nap, stumbled down the steps, catching herself by grabbing for the rail. She caught her breath while looking back up the stairs. If she wasn't fully awake before, she definitely was awake now. The house was quiet with Juan gone off running errands. He didn't even wake her to let her know he was going out. She entered the kitchen looking for something to snack on. A bowl of cereal would do. She grabbed her bowl of cereal and headed to the living room. She put her bowl down once she saw blue and red lights flickering out her window. She stood there paralyzed with fear. The door flung in with a stream of police officers yelling at her. Her body shifted violently as Detective Santiago spun her around, placing handcuffs on her wrists. She never said a word, she didn't hear anything but a harsh ringing noise in her ears.

Noemi lowered her as she climbed into the patrol car. The seat was hard and plastic, and her hands barely grazed the back as she stared out the window. As the car pulled away and approached the entrance to her street, she caught sight of Jasmine standing in front of a car, flipping her the bird.

Noemi sat in silence.

Two hours later Juan stood with his arms crossed unable to see Noemi. He waited for their attorney to come out and update him. He watched a tall woman nod at him then walk up to him. "Are you Mrs. Watson?"

"Yes, please just call me Wanda. I saw your wife and she is doing fine. I met with the detective and they are charging her with murder and some other charges."

Juan leaned against the wall just gutted and flabbergasted. "Murder?"

"She's the murder suspect for the young man, Chance Wright."

"She didn't kill him. None of our vehicles were part of any hit and run."

"There's some evidence I have to review but I will be back to sit with your wife when she is being questioned again. Why did she have Chance's belongings? The police recovered some things from their search. I will touch base with you tomorrow."

Juan watched Mrs. Watson walk away, puzzled by the sight of a box in the garage he had never noticed before. Why hadn't the police taken it when they executed the search warrant? He realized he had no choice but to head home; there was nothing more he could do for Noemi here.

Chapter 65

• • • •

BRENT STOOD NEXT TO Jasmine as she had a sudden need to mutter her thoughts in a harried way. She was elated over the arrest of Noemi but concerned about the charges not sticking. Jasmine caught Brent looking confused and slightly withdrawn in his own thoughts. "Sorry about unloading all of my manic thoughts on you."

Brent's chest rose with a deep inhalation. "So you said she was charged with murder? Wouldn't that be like a negligent driver or manslaughter kind of thing?"

"Based off of the evidence they have and what witnesses have said, they think she had motive."

"To hurt you? Chance was just an innocent bystander."

"That has to be determined but she definitely didn't like me. If she was harassing Chance and he rebuffed her, she could've just went after him. I don't know, all I know is my child is dead and I believe Noemi is behind it all. She had my son's belongings like some trophy collection. She was definitely a nut job."

"This is a lot. I hope you get some peace of mind."

Jasmine coughed into the crook of her arm. "I'm going to get more than that. Trust me on that."

• • • •

ZOYA PRESSED HER FACE into the freshly cleaned towel, a floral scent wafted around her nostrils. She spun around quickly to the front door opening. "Hey, who just came in the house?"

Leonard came around the corner to the laundry room. "Just me."

"You are home early."

"Yeah, today was kind of bonkers but I'm home. Where is Aalia?"

"She's by Sophie's house. Why was today crazy?"

"One of the victims from that accident involving the teacher died."

Zoya dropped the towel on the floor, her jaw dropped open as well. "What?"

"Yes, their injuries were all over the place and they were stable then all of a sudden there were complications. They were rushed to surgery and coded."

"Oh my goodness. You think they will go after Noemi?"

"I don't see why not. They have to prove that the death occurred due to the injuries incurred from the accident, and I don't see why that can't be proven. That accident was bad. Noemi is lucky to be alive."

Zoya felt her phone vibrate in her cardigans pocket. She reached for her phone seeing Aalia's face smiling up at her. She quickly accepted the call on speaker. "Hey honey."

"Mom, they arrested Mrs. Jimenez. They are charging her with murder."

Chapter 66

••••

ZOYA SAT OPPOSITE MARLENE while the girls chatted amongst themselves. Zoya stared off at the TV, her thoughts a bit scattered, she got up to get a bottle of wine. "You guys hungry? Pizza?" She grabbed wine glasses and a bottle of wine then headed back to her spot on the couch. She watched Marlene place the order for the pizzas. "How did Jasmine sound when she called you?"

Marlene looked up from her phone. "She was rather calm but you could tell she felt overwhelmed. I mean this is huge. I just about dropped my phone when she said it. She was so blunt about it. Brent was with her. Oh, and she was there when they arrested her. The detective gave her the heads up."

"Wow and yikes all at the same time." Zoya passed Marlene a full glass of wine. "The girls are handling all of this pretty well. Wait until this hits the school. I wonder what evidence finally made the police make the arrest?"

"That's a good question. There's just so much going against her but what about the truck?"

"Anything is possible, she could've had access to a truck or the police discovered something that really ties her to the incident." Zoya's eyes trailed the profile of her daughter's face.

Aalia feeling someone staring at her turned to look at her mother, she smiled, hiding her true feelings. She was devastated by the news of her teacher's arrest and still believes she had no part in harming anyone, much less Chance. She leaned forward tapping Sophie's knee. "This isn't right. We can't accept this for her. She didn't do anything."

Sophie played with her ring, oscillating between feeling sympathy and believing the worst. "I don't know. There's nothing we can do anyway."

"We can get to the bottom of this."

"How, we are just two girls in high school. We are not the police."

"Maybe we can find something to exonerate her."

Sophie knowing Aalia wouldn't let this go, nodded halfheartedly. "Really, I think our mother's will be nosy enough to do some poking around. I don't think we even have to ask nicely."

"See, I knew you would get it."

Chapter 67

••••

ZOYA CRUMPLED THE PAPER before tossing it in the trash. She stood with Marlene in the hallway outside of the front office. News of Noemi's arrest had spread quickly throughout the school, prompting several parents to approach Mr. Walker with their questions. Zoya nudged Marlene who looked more annoyed than normal. "I didn't tell you, one of the people involved in the accident died."

"No!"

"Yup!"

"She can't catch a break."

Zoya bit her bottom lip. "Hi, girls."

Aalia and Sophie casually walked up to their mothers. "We need your help. Mrs. Jimenez did not kill Chance. We need to prove her innocence." Aalia looked at Sophie who didn't look convinced of their teacher's innocence.

"Girls, I don't think there is anything we can do." Marlene's left eye twitched. "But what do you got?"

Aalia, seeing an ally in her endeavors, smiled broadly. "Okay, so they have to prove that Mrs. Jimenez ran them off the road."

"I think they have a motive. They haven't tracked down the vehicle or the driver who ran them off the road."

"Well, can you two talk to Mrs. Wright and get some details? Like, how are they holding Mrs. Jimenez...with what evidence?" Aalia placed her hands in a prayer position, pleading for a little help.

Marlene tapped her foot as she saw Mr. Walker out patrolling the hall. "As nosey as I am, I don't think talking to Jasmine will get anything you can use to free Mrs. Jimenez. Jasmine is the last person to offer anything to help Mrs. Jimenez. But now that I think about it, I would love to know what they pinged Mrs. Jimenez on."

••••

DETECTIVE SANTIAGO sat with Mrs. Watson showing her the evidence they had against Mrs. Jimenez. They were waiting for Mrs. Jimenez to be brought to the interrogation room. As if on cue, the door flew open and Noemi was escorted in.

Mrs. Watson sat next to Noemi, not giving a hint of what she saw. "We can begin."

Detective Santiago didn't need to be told but one time. He was ready. "You were asked to leave the fundraiser due to Mrs. Wright being there, you didn't leave. You sat in the parking lot and left only after you saw Mrs. Wright leave. We found pieces of the Wright's vehicle in your garage."

Noemi shook her head vigorously. "I didn't hit them. I don't know what you are talking about." She watched Detective Santiago place plastic bags filled with fragments of a car. He pointed at another bag that had broken pieces of a taillight and some unrecognizable parts. "Why were these in your garage?"

Noemi sat in silence not sure of how to respond.

Detective Santiago then pulled out another box and started putting Chance's personal items on the table. "This box was found in your garage too. Why do you have a collection of Chance's stuff?"

"I don't know...my garage?"

"It was well known at the school that you had a tense relationship with Mrs. Wright, then there are the allegations that you were trying to have an inappropriate relationship with her son. He didn't respond the way you wanted, and you then harassed him by using your authority as his teacher. Picking on him, giving him low grades, getting him kicked off his sports teams."

"No, there was no relationship. I was just his teacher. He was not putting in the effort and was graded appropriately."

"Do you deny following Mrs. Wright from the school after she left the fundraiser?"

Sweat began to trickle down Noemi's forehead as she blinked a few times, feeling the room start to spin around her. "I did follow her but she was going in the direction I needed to go. I got stopped at a light and by the time I was passing the lake, the accident had already happened. I didn't even know it was her car down there. People had pulled over to the side and I kept on driving home."

"Maybe you had someone else hit her car? Maybe you were following them to make sure the accident happened?"

Mrs. Watson tapped the table with her pen. "You are making assumptions...no fact."

Detective Santiago started to pack away the evidence he had so eloquently displayed on the table. "No problem...we will get to the bottom of this. I'm done...for now."

Chapter 68

••••

ZOYA WIPED HER NOSE with a tissue before grabbing the tray of lasagna. She watched Marlene hold the door open for her. Jasmine peeked around the corner, waving her in. "Jasmine, how are you doing?"

Jasmine smiled, her hair styled in a neat bun. She managed to summon enough energy to apply some makeup. "It's so good to see you two. A lot has been going on. I got to catch you all up."

Zoya handed Jasmine the tray of lasagna. Marlene took the breadsticks and salad to the kitchen. Marlene grabbed plates from Jasmine and started to dish out food for everyone. "We heard that Mrs. Jimenez got arrested."

Jasmine chewed on croutons as she nodded in agreement. "She sure did. I was there to witness it. They found some of Chance's personal belongings as well as pieces of my car in her garage. Like trophies, I tell you. Sick bastard."

Marlene swallowed her bite of lasagna. "Wait...they found what in her garage? Well, that does seem suspicious."

Jasmine shook a bottle of wine at the ladies. "Glasses are in the cupboard behind you. Yes, so she's in jail. Why have my son's things? Why have pieces of my car...they still don't have the vehicle that hit us, but they are thinking she had help. Maybe her husband. Who knows."

"You think her husband helped her?"

"I really don't know what to think. She had to have told him about all of our back-and-forth disagreements. Then, to hear that his wife was being inappropriate with a student...my son. That could have triggered him."

Marlene drank the rest of her wine, pointing at the bottle for more. "Good grief, I didn't think about that."

Jasmine finished her food. The wine was going to her head quicker than normal. "Right, so Detective Santiago will get to the bottom of this. He will be questioning folks soon enough."

Zoya covered her mouth with her hand. "One of the people in the accident she caused, died."

Jasmine's eyes flickered with renewed energy. She chuckled and snorted. "I heard about that. That family is going to add that to their lawsuit." Her nose crinkled as she cackled. "Oh, pardon me. I feel awful for the family, but Mrs. Jimenez is going to pay for all that she has done. How many lives has she ruined?"

Chapter 69

••••

AALIA STOOD BY HER cone waiting for her mother's car to pull up. She arched her back, feeling the weight of her backpack starting to take its toll. Today she was glad to be in her gym uniform, she was not prepared for the chill in the air. Her mother told her to get her coat, but she thought she could handle it. Aalia waved at Sophie who was a few cones away, then she was joined by Brent Jr. He stood next to her, play fighting with a classmate. Aalia saw her mom's car roll to a stop in front of her. She got in quickly to get out of the cold.

Zoya pointed at Aalia's backpack. "That looks heavy. I told you to wear a coat."

Aalia, ignoring her mom's coat jab, looked behind her at Brent. "Didn't his dad have a truck?"

Zoya looked in her rear view mirror at Brent and his dad. "I never really paid attention to their vehicle. I think he has a work car. He's a realtor, you know. Him and Jasmine show some of the same homes."

"He had a truck. He has been using this car for a while now."

"Yes. I think you are right."

Aalia closed her eyes in thought. As soon as she got home, she grabbed a snack, changed her clothes, and waited for Sophie to pick her up. They were going to a friend's birthday dinner. She grabbed her cell phone them headed out to Sophie and Marlene. "Hi!"

Sophie squealed with excitement. "This is going to be fun. I have the gift."

The girls chatted and laughed throughout the entire ride. When they arrive at the restaurant, they left Marlene to search for a parking space. Aalia and Sophie quickly dashed into the bustling group of teens and found their seats. As they settled in, Aalia brushed her arm against Brent Jr. "Oh sorry."

Brent smiled brushing off her apology. "Aalia, right?"

Aalia, shocked that he even knew her name, blushed. "Yes."

"Nice to meet you."

"Didn't your dad have a truck, like a huge one?"

"Yes."

"I haven't seen it in weeks."

Brent grabbed the breadbasket, snagging a roll then handed the basket to Aalia. "It's at home. He uses it a little less now."

Aalia chewed on her bread, feeling a bit out of place. "Life is different without Chance around. He used to bother you a lot."

"That is one person I don't miss. He just was mean for no reason. I never did anything to him."

Aalia mingled with a few other people who were within earshot of her. The birthday dinner was entertaining. Aalia and Sophie grabbed their purses and headed out of the restaurant. They met Marlene out front. "Brent is really nice."

Sophie plucked fuzz off of her sweater. "Yes, he is. He's quiet from what I've seen."

"I asked about his dad's truck. He says his dad doesn't use it as much now. That was his main vehicle and now he doesn't use it. Marlene? If you had an opportunity to see their truck, you think you would know if that was the truck that hit the Wright's car?"

Marlene honked her horn at a car that stopped short. "Maybe, but I don't think Brent Sr. had anything to do with that. They are friends with Jasmine."

"Correction...Brent Sr. is friends with Jasmine." Aalia chuckled to herself.

"But...but, Brent offered to take Jasmine home after the fundraiser. He stayed afterwards to help with cleanup."

"Are you sure about that? You and Mom left."

"I'm pretty sure but who knows. Once we left, anything could've happened."

Chapter 70

• • • •

JASMINE FOLDED CLOTHES as she watched the news. Today was a good day, she sold a home, drafted all the documents for another closing, and touched base with Zoya. Now that her chore list was complete and there were no pressing actions to derail her, she ventured back to her laptop to do some research. After having a thorough conversation with Detective Santiago, she had confirmed Noemi's attorney's identity. Not only had she retrieved the information from the sign-up sheet at the home Brent was showing, but it was also Brent who informed her of the connection.

Jasmine's mind swirled with ideas on how she could use this to her advantage. She glanced at her phone, what perfect timing for Brent to give her a call. "I was just thinking of you."

"I hope it was good thoughts." Brent huffed.

"When are you going to meet with your client, the attorney?"

"She's not my client per se, Cindy is on maternity leave so I took Mrs. Watson on."

"I hope she finds what she's looking for."

"She will, she really liked that one house on Bart Street."

Jasmine smiled slyly to herself. "Keep me posted on that." Jasmine ended the call, she needed to get back to her research.

• • • •

NOEMI WAS NOT DOING well in jail. There was no way she was being released anytime soon. She gathered her notebook then followed the guard to the conference room where she could meet with Mrs. Watson. It had been a week since their last meeting, and no news couldn't be good news. As soon as she saw Mrs. Watson, a warm smile spread across her face. "Hello."

Mrs. Watson set a bag on the table alongside two coffees. "Hi. Juan told me what coffee you like, he gave me your medication and sent this lovely casserole."

Noemi grabbed the spoon and started eating. "Thank you. So weird, Juan doesn't know how to make this dish. I guess he has to practice more cooking since I'm not there. He makes great steaks and potatoes."

"Well, maybe we can get you home. I'm trying to see if you can be released on bond."

"We don't have the money."

"Don't get discouraged, let's at least obtain the option and work out the money later."

"Okay. I understand." Noemi inhaled the food and drank all of her coffee. She sat and talked with Mrs. Watson for a good half hour then it was time to go back to her cell. She shuffled down the hall, her belly full, her spirits lifted, and feeling a bit lighter in mood.

Barely situated on her bed, she felt a sharp pain in her stomach. She passed it off as cramps and made herself go to sleep. An hour later, she threw the thin blanket off herself, covered in sweat, the cramps had her doubled over. She violently vomited, the smell permeated the small room quickly. Her eyes glazed over as she passed out.

Chapter 71

• • • •

JASMINE SAT IN THE hospital parking lot listening to Brent's scattered stream of consciousness. "Slow down, what's the problem?"

Brent tried to collect his thoughts. "It's Brent! He was knocked out cold at his game. We are in the ER."

"What? I'm at the hospital too. Someone may have broken his toe. Craig...not me." Jasmine gathered her purse and coat and rushed back to the ER. She noticed Craig was no longer in the waiting room so she went to the nurse. After a quick rundown she was escorted to Craig's bed. She looked around and could see Brent across the room. She told Craig she would be back and pulled his curtain closed. She quickly rounded the nursing station and whispered at the curtain. The curtain slid back and there was Brent looking frazzled. "Hey, you two all right?"

Brent gave Jasmine a side hug. "He has to get an MRI."

Jasmine noticing some excited commotion looked in disbelief as police officers came streaming in the ER with a patient. "I wonder what that is all about?" She peered back at Brent. "I should get back to Craig. Keep me posted." Jasmine made her way back to Craig and closed his curtain. All the commotion was now happening in the curtained off bay next to them. Jasmine sat down while Craig dozed off. She looked at his swollen left foot. Definitely a broken bone in there somewhere. Jasmine's ears perked up as she listened to the police officers talking to someone. She craned her head to hear better. She heard Juan's name and knew it was Noemi lying in that bed. She fought the urge to bolt over there. She bit her tongue and kept herself beside her husband. She was in no rush to leave the ER now.

A few hours later Jasmine was now in Noemi's hospital room. Jasmine grabbed gloves from the table, pulling them back nice and snug. She grabbed the pocketknife from her pocket, placing it securely in Noemi's hand. She ripped out the I.V. tube out of Noemi's arm and disconnected her from the monitors. She then grabbed a pillow, placing it over Noemi's face, she held it firmly as Noemi struggled. Jasmine fell back as Noemi sat up, but she quickly smiled and got back on her feet. Playfully, she pushed the table forward toward Noemi and then made a mad dash for the door screaming. "She has a knife!"

Jasmine slipped off the gloves, placing them in her pocket as the police officer ran back to Noemi's room. Yelling and screams echoed through the floor. Jasmine flinched when she heard a gunshot, she laughed when she heard the second shot. She returned to the orthopedic floor that Craig was on. Turned out he needed surgery so that extended her hospital stay.

Jasmine reached for her phone, she wanted to check on Brent Jr. She smiled broadly as Brent Sr. appeared on her screen. "Hey there, how is your son doing?"

Brent turned the phone to show his son playing a video game. "Normal as you can see. You guys holding up?"

"Yeah, surgery was a success, I guess. He has some plate on his foot. Mr. Bionic guy over here."

"You look great. All smiles."

Jasmine laughed awkwardly. "I feel great. Nothing like being in the hospital. I think I'm going to hit the cafeteria up for a snack."

"Yes, get some food. When will Craig be released?"

"Tomorrow. I get another night to hang out here." Jasmine thought about having some carrot cake. She deserved a treat after all.

Chapter 72

AALIA STARED AT THE news in disbelief. A shooting at the hospital her father worked at. She screamed for her mother. "Mom! Mom!"

Zoya ran into Aalia's room wrapped in a towel, her hair still wet and full of shampoo. "What?" Her eyes followed her daughter's gaze to the TV. She clutched the towel in one hand and grabbed Aalia's phone with the other. She quickly dialed her husband's number. Several rings passed and then his voicemail message came on. She continued to look at the TV as the phone vibrated in her hand. Daddy flashed across the screen. "What is going on? Are you safe?"

Leonard quickly shouted commands to a nurse then brought his attention back to Zoya. "I'm fine. A prisoner was shot. I think it was Noemi. She has to be in surgery by now. The hospital is sort of locked down. They are diverting ER patients to other hospitals. Listen, I will call you later."

"Noemi...shot!" Zoya grabbed Aalia, giving her a secure shake and hug. "Dad's fine." Zoya looked at herself in the mirror and went back to finish washing her hair.

SOPHIE GLARED AT HER tablet in disbelief, unable to process what she was seeing. Someone had posted footage of people running for cover while police swarmed the hospital. It was all happening to fast for her to handle. Frantically, she grabbed her phone and texted Aalia to check on her dad. Fortunately he was okay. "Mom, you hear about the hospital being on lockdown?"

Marlene dropped her fork, the clanking noise echoed throughout the kitchen. "Leonard?"

"He's fine."

Marlene grabbed her keys. "Let's go."

Sophie and Marlene walked around the corner to get to Zoya's house. Marlene pushed the doorbell, waved at the camera, then turned the doorknob. "Hello!" Her arms already open as she saw Aalia scampering down the stairs.

She hugged her then planted a kiss on her forehead. "I'm glad your dad is safe. He's busy being a hero."

Zoya quickly descended down the stairs. "Well, I got some interesting text messages from Jasmine. She's in the hospital, her husband broke his foot and needed surgery. Anyway, Noemi was shot."

Marlene directed the girls to the living room. "Why was she in the hospital?"

"I'm not sure why she was there, some medical emergency. Oh, and the McGregors are there too."

Chapter 73

••••

BRENT SR. SAT AT THE end of his son's bed, watching the news. In the morning they could go home. Brent Jr. had a concussion and needed to rest. The hospital was no longer under a lockdown, but everyone was still skittish. Brent looked at his watch, then updated his wife. He turned to the soft knocking on the door. "Come in." He knew it was Jasmine taking a break from sitting with Craig. "Crazy day, right?"

"Can you believe it?"

"I wonder what happened, you know, what led up to her getting shot."

Jasmine smiled as she watched the TV. "We may never know. I wonder how she's doing?" Jasmine grabbed her phone sending Zoya quick updates. "I know a doctor here, he's one of the kids' dads. You know Zoya? Her husband. He actually treated me and my son that horrible night."

"Oh really? Maybe he knows how she is doing."

"I plan on finding out." Jasmine sent her queries to Zoya. "How's Brent?"

"We go home tomorrow. He will be taking a break from sports, getting rest, and reducing his activities."

••••

ZOYA LISTENED TO THE whirring sound of the garage door opening. Leonard was home. It was after midnight, he would normally be home hours ago. Zoya quickly slipped out of bed, pushing her feet into her fluffy slippers, wrapping a throw blanket around her shoulders, and headed downstairs. She ran into Leonard's arms, burying her face in his chest.

"I'm good. Another dramatic day at the Emergency Room. Well, the hospital. The ER was relatively quiet today."

Zoya tucked her long bangs behind her ear. "How is she, Noemi?"

"Critical condition. I don't know how she got out of her restraints but she did, and she was brandishing a weapon. She was shot twice, one bullet in her thigh and the other in the abdomen."

"Wow, that's a lot. Do you know one of the doctor's on that floor?"

"Dr. Lang was up there, and I know a couple of the nurses up there. This information came swirling through the nosey staff network. There will probably be some in-house meeting and email sent out."

Zoya shrugged her shoulders. "I was texting with Jasmine. She and Brent are still at the hospital."

"What a coincidence. I think they were both in the ER when Noemi came in. The world makes crazy connections." Leonard jogged down the hall to the bathroom. He needed to take a shower before going to bed.

Chapter 74

••••

AALIA SAT NEXT TO SOPHIE in the gymnasium, watching students play basketball. It was a chaotic free-for-all, an indoor recess day due to the rain. Aalia spotted Brent chatting with his friends, when he suddenly looked up and waved at her. Startled, se glanced around, wondering if he was waving at her. When she realized he was, she waved back, and he smiled. "Okay." Aalia grabbed Sophie's hand, dragging her over to where Brent was. "Hey, I heard you were in the hospital a few days ago."

Brent smiled as he pointed to his head. "Concussion. There was a lot going on and I barely remember half of it. One of these morons knocked me out during the game."

Aalia gathered her cardigan around her. "You were there when the hospital got locked down. My dad works in the ER."

Brent clapped his hands after seeing one of his friends throw a ball across the gym. "Yes, I was kind of zoned out through that. My floor was quiet. Your dad was fine, right?"

"Yes, he was good. That was scary, though." Aalia turned to look at Sophie who was barely paying attention. "It's good to see you and hope you feel better."

Sophie took out some gum, offering everyone some. "You live near Lake Whetstone?"

Brent shook his head. "Yeah, you guys live on the other side. I've seen your cars turn at the intersection."

"Yup, there's a few of us in that neighborhood. We all live in the same area. Did you know Mrs. Jimenez used to live in our neighborhood?"

"I did, but only because my dad is her realtor. She lives on my side now. Crazy, huh?"

"Small world." Sophie smiled broadly. "Is your dad helping with the backdrop for the play?"

"Yes, he is. He's always building something."

"Well, my mom is helping too. Maybe we will see each other." Sophie grabbed Aalia, taking her to the front door. The kids were lining up to head back to their classrooms. "You should thank me."

Aalia rolled her eyes as she giggled. "For what?"

"I just got you inside the McGregor house."

• • • •

MARLENE, ZOYA, AND the girls pulled up to the McGregor house. They had several bolts of fabric and tools. Marlene quickly handed off items to Brent Sr. "Sorry for being late. All of a sudden, the girls wanted to help."

Brent led the group to his shed where all the construction work happened. He laid out one bolt of fabric and started draping the material to a bench. "Girls, why don't you go find Brent Jr. He's probably in the basement, playing some video game."

Aalia and Sophie walked back through the back yard up to the basement door. Right on schedule, Brent opened the door for them. "Your dad sent us to find you."

Brent ushered the girls into his playroom, offered them sodas and snacks. "Once my dad gets going, he's in the zone. He really likes building stuff."

Aalia coughed as soda went down the wrong pipe. She wiped her mouth quickly. "Your dad did a lot for the Casino Night. I remember seeing you helping him kind of set up."

"That was brutal. He built some heavy pieces. Chance tried to sucker punch me but my dad came around the corner. You should've seen Chance's face when he saw my dad. He ran out of there so quick."

"Everyone had to pass Lake Whetstone."

Sophie looked at Brent just as confused as he was. "What?"

Aalia put her soda on the table. "Everyone had to pass the lake. Mrs. Jimenez lives over on that side. She wasn't following Mrs. Wright. She was just going in the same direction to get home. Brent, when your dad got home, he had to pass the accident."

Brent scratched his head still a bit confused. "I don't really remember when my dad got home. I went to bed. My mom would've been up."

"Why didn't your mom go to the fundraiser?"

"My mom is not into those things. She doesn't like all the people and she considers most of the parents as fake. My mom's weird. She doesn't like social events."

"Oh." Aalia never saw Brent's mom. "Is your mom here?"

"No, she's at her store."

"She has a store? Cool."

"She's a caterer but she makes cakes. Cakes are her passion."

Aalia rubbed her knees, mimicking the way her mom does when she's deep in thought.

Chapter 75

AALIA PULLED OUT HER tablet and started a search of Brent's mom. A few minutes in and she found pictures of Mrs. McGregor outside of her store, photos with her son and social media promotions. She looked happy. All this time and Aalia was seeing the woman for the first time.

Sophie looked at the screen then went back to watching the TV. "I wonder if she ever had to deal with Chance?"

"Or his mom?"

Sophie opened the bag of chips and started eating. "I think Mr. McGregor handled everything where Chance was concerned. I've never seen this lady."

Aalia zoomed in on a photo with the whole McGregor family standing in front of a large catering truck. She stuffed her feet in her fluffy slippers then headed downstairs to talk to her mom and Marlene. "Ladies, look at this."

Zoya stared at the photo, her brows furrowed in concentration. "Who is this?"

"That's Brent's mom." Aalia offered up the information like a prize. "Look at the catering truck, it has the school magnet on it and it's a big truck."

Marlene grabbed the phone, her jaw went slack. "Wait, they catered the fundraiser."

Zoya cocked her neck to the side, giving Marlene a good stare down. "Really?"

Marlene smiled at Aalia. "You are thinking something."

Aalia's eyes widened as she saw her opportunity to draw Marlene in further down the rabbit hole. "Now, Mrs. McGregor has a truck, was this the vehicle you saw that night?"

Marlene looked at Zoya skeptical of the potential response. "When we viewed the camera footage it was a truck but remember the footage wasn't the best."

"But didn't we say the truck had the school decal on it?" Zoya corrected her posture as she tried to remember the details.

Aalia leaned against the couch, her arms crossed, and her mind reeling with ideas. "Like I told Brent last night. Everyone had to pass the lake. The

McGregor's have trucks and more than one based on this picture. The detective needs to check their vehicles out. I'm not saying murder, but it was an accident and Mrs. Jimenez is innocent."

Sophie came prancing down the stairs and up to the group. "Mrs. Jimenez had incriminating evidence."

"We need to find the truck that ran the Wrights off the road. I bet when that is found, they will see that Mrs. Jimenez had no connection. She was just going home."

Marlene grabbed her phone. "I guess there's no harm in telling the detective this." Marlene found Detective Santiago in her contact list.

"Wait!" Zoya grabbed the phone and ended the call. "If you call and open up a can of worms, Brent will know. I don't think we should rock the boat. We don't want to accuse people."

Marlene didn't think that far out, this is why she needed Zoya's cool mind to slow her down. All eyes looked at her ringing phone. Detective Santiago was calling. Now what?

Chapter 76

• • • •

DETECTIVE SANTIAGO watched the Cakes On Us store front for an hour. He had been to the back of the store and didn't see the catering truck. He wasn't sure how many catering trucks they had but it didn't seem to be a lot. So far, he saw Mrs. McGregor and another lady. No catering truck in the parking lot. Mrs. McGregor left the store with a package, maybe a cake. She got into a car and drove off.

Detective Santiago got out of his car, strolled up to the store and walked in posing as a customer. "Hey there, I'm new to the area and I could've sworn I saw your company truck."

Alice walked up to the counter with a smile. "You probably have. We got two delivery vans. Well, one van and there's a truck."

"How many of y'all work here?"

"It's just me and Ingrid. Ingrid is the owner."

"Oh, so just you two. Where's the delivery trucks?"

"You know what? The van is probably with Ingrid. She uses it as her personal vehicle too. As for the truck, I think it's with her husband. I haven't seen it for a few weeks now. We haven't had big deliveries since the fundraiser so it's not missed."

"You all do fundraisers? Just cakes?"

Alice wiped down the counter until it gleamed. "Just a misconception," She said. "We also do catering. We prepare meals and cakes. We just landed a big job at the Catholic high school. We loaded up the truck and van with everything we need-cooking elements, trays, plates-you name it, we've got it."

"That's amazing. Can I have a card?"

Alice produced a card and pamphlet. "I will do you one better...here's a coupon for being a first-time customer. We do cupcakes. Cater parties. Check out our website too." Alice bagged a few chocolate chip cookies. "Here you go."

"Oh, you are too kind."

"I'm Alice. If you got a need for sweets come on in."

"I most definitely will. In my line of work, we love sweets." Detective Santiago took a bite of a cookie, it was soft and the chocolate was still warm and gooey. He smiled as he went back to his car. He needed to swing by the McGregor house and see what they were up to.

Chapter 77

• • • •

DETECTIVE SANTIAGO stood with Mrs. McGregor in front of the garage. His gaze caught a blue tarp draped across the front of the truck. He pointed at the truck. "May I take a look?" He walked past her to inspect the vehicle. He removed the tarp seeing the hood gone and the engine missing but no damage to the truck. He quickly put the tarp back as he found it. "So where's the other truck?"

Ingrid threw her hands in the air disgusted at the mere thought of her delivery truck. "The transmission went on that truck. I'm so annoyed. I may as well buy another truck, the price to fix the transmission is astronomical." Ingrid watched Detective Santiago exit the garage.

"It's at a shop getting fixed?"

"No, my brother has it while I decide what I want to do. I may just have to use my van for a while."

"What's going on with this truck?"

Ingrid looked at Brent's truck, she laughed through her annoyance. "My husband swears he will get that back up and running. He is a fixer. Just takes time. He has parts coming in and he will get her back on the road. Maybe I should use his truck and get rid of mine." Ingrid waved at the mailman as she walked down the driveway. "I got to go, I have cakes to make. I can't keep Alice waiting."

• • • •

JASMINE SAT ACROSS from Mrs. Watson, she admired her amber jacket. Her fingers glided across her phone as she kept watch. She tapped her ear as if answering a call. "Hi, Mr. Jimenez, I was checking in on your wife, Noemi. I will be representing her. I know this is a difficult time, but our firm will do everything we can to see you all through this." Jasmine tapped at her screen, nodded her head then ended the call. She looked up at Mrs. Watson who by now was staring right back at her. "Can I help you?"

Mrs. Watson blinked a few times. "You look familiar, but I can't place you. You know the Jimenez family?"

"Oh, I don't know them, they are clients. They have some legal issues."

Mrs. Watson shook her head. "Yes."

"You know, there was an incident at the hospital involving her, she's in critical condition but hopefully she makes a speedy recovery. You are her attorney aren't you? I knew I recognized you."

Mrs. Watson leaned forward to shake Jasmine's hand. "Yes, I am."

Jasmine rummaged through her purse, her hair fell in front of her face as she pulled out a scarf which had a small pocketknife entangled in it. The pocketknife skidded across the floor stopping by Mrs. Watson's brown suede pumps. "Oh my, could be a dear soul and grab that for me?" Jasmine quickly pushed her purse in Mrs. Watson's direction.

Mrs. Watson grabbed the pocketknife and placed it in Jasmine's purse. She watched Jasmine stuff the scarf back in the purse. "It was nice talking to you."

Jasmine closed her purse as she started to make her exit. "Good luck."

Chapter 78

• • • •

BRENT TOSSED A BEER to Jake, they both had a good laugh over the spilled oil now glistening on his garage floor. Together they moved the hoisted engine over the truck, lowering it back into place. After hooking everything up and throwing back a few more beers, it was time to see if the truck would start. Brent got in, turned the key, and the truck roared back to life. He threw his one free hand in the air triumphantly. "Let me take her for a spin, be right back."

Jake dropped powder on the oil, then finished his beer. "Hey, sis!"

Ingrid punched her brother in the arm, spun away from him, then landed another playful jab on him. "What about my truck?"

Jake mustered up a brilliant smile. "I got you! You will get her back by the end of the week. I'm even going to give her a good detailing job. She's gonna look like new."

• • • •

MRS. WATSON HELD NOEMI'S hand, a smile spread across her face. "Now, can you tell me what happened? The police are saying you had a knife, you came at the police and wouldn't follow their commands."

Noemi tried to raise her hand but it was shackled to the bed rail. "Listen to me. I don't really recall much of anything. I just know I woke up here. How did I even get here?"

"You got very ill at the jail and were found unconscious. That's the initial reason. Then you were moved to a regular floor for observation and got shot when the police were trying to restrain you. I can probably say you were under the influence of medication and didn't know what you were doing? We have a big mountain to climb."

"I really wish I could end all of this. This is a nightmare."

"Stay positive. Let me work my magic."

Noemi slept uncomfortably for a couple hours. She woke up with dinner already set up on her tray. As she took her first bite, a nurse entered her room checking her vitals.

The nurse snapped her gloved fingers before making sure her mask was fitting just right. "Mrs. Jimenez, on a scale of one to ten, what would you say your pain level is?"

Noemi shifted forward to get another bite of food in. "I would say a seven." She could feel her wounds as they rubbed against the bandages and gauze.

The nurse chuckled as she pulled back Noemi's blanket exposing her thigh. The sound of the compression machine hummed from the foot of the bed. In a sudden move, she drew a pocketknife and sliced into Noemi's leg. Dropping the knife beside Noemi's leg, she fled the room. As she rushed out, the piercing sound of Noemi's agonized screams echoed in her ears.

Jasmine quickly left the hospital. As soon as she got to the garage, she got in her car, took off the surgical gloves, tossed them in a plastic bag sitting on the passenger seat, started the car and drove off. She took off her mask, breathing deeply. She got home, quickly taking off the scrubs she recently bought and tossed them in the trash along with the plastic bag. She took a quick shower, making sure to scrub herself down. Once she got dressed and felt comfortable, she went to check on Craig. "How are you doing?"

Craig pointed at his booted foot. "No complaints. I can't wait until my foot heals. Where did you run off to?"

"I had to check on a friend. I have to make sure people are held accountable."

Craig hobbled across the room to retrieve his phone. "I got to call the office, but I think we should order in tonight."

Jasmine nodded in agreement then left the room. She grabbed a glass to get some water. Under no circumstances was Noemi leaving that hospital. Jasmine had all the time in the world to handle Noemi.

Chapter 79

• • • •

BRENT STOOD NEXT TO Ingrid setting up one of her mixers. "Sorry to be a nag, but who came here asking about your truck?"

Ingrid dropped a stick of butter in the mixer then turned it on. She cracked some eggs and dropped them into the mixing bowl. "I can't remember a name. Tall guy."

"You just let a stranger into our garage?"

"No, he was a stranger to me, but he knew Alice. He said Alice had told him that our truck was out of commission. He wanted to see the truck."

Brent scratched his head, perplexed with how Ingrid just let some random guy into the garage. "Why did he want to see the truck? Explain to me how he approached you."

Ingrid searched the cupboard for her vanilla extract. "I was already outside, bringing stuff into the garage. In all honesty, I was struggling to bring in a table, I heard him coming up the driveway offering to help. He said he had talked to Alice and he really liked the cookies. He helped me, and while we were talking, he mentioned the truck and that he had seen it. You know I just assumed he saw it when my brother was driving it. I told him it's not working right now. Nice guy. I had to get back to making an order and he left."

Brent rocked back and forth still contemplating who came to the house. Whoever it was, they knew Alice and she wouldn't send a crazy person to his house.

• • • •

DETECTIVE SANTIAGO stood in front of Mr. Jimenez taking notes. Noemi couldn't catch a break. "Mr. Jimenez, I spoke with the nurses and the officer that was stationed outside of her room. They said the only people to see her today were you and her attorney, Mrs. Watson. They recovered this pocketknife which I'm taking to have dusted for prints. Do you know how she acquired this? Does this belong to you?"

Juan shrugged his shoulders, the stress of everything weighing him down. "That's not ours. I don't know how or why? You know Noemi was telling Mrs.

Watson that she wanted this to end it all, you think she was being suicidal? How could she do this?"

"We will get to the bottom of this. You said she mentioned potentially harming herself to your attorney? I will talk to her."

"Thank you, I know you think my wife is the main suspect but I'm telling you, she didn't do it. Right now, I feel like she is being framed."

"Who would frame her?"

"I know this is going to sound terrible but that Jasmine lady. I know her son is gone. She's been through a lot but she never liked my wife. She would do anything in her power to get back at her."

"Mrs. Wright and her son are the victims."

"Well, she is spiteful and could be using her son's tragedy to make my wife the suspect. Look into that."

Detective Santiago watched Noemi being wheeled into the recovery room. She needed more than stitches to repair her leg. That had to be one gnarly gash. Detective Santiago placed the bag with the pocketknife in an evidence bag and made his way out of the hospital.

Chapter 80

MRS. WATSON PASSED the water bottle to Detective Santiago, she placed her laptop on the table to take some notes. "I wanted to review some of the evidence so I'm glad I ran into you. Have you gotten any more details about this mysterious truck?"

Detective Santiago glanced at his notes. "We have had some new leads that look promising. We know the make and model based off of the evidence gathered, but you must wonder why these parts were found in the Jimenez's possession."

"I can't speak on that. Can I review photos from the scene of the accident?"

Detective Santiago handed the file over. He watched her as she went through each photo. Her gaze grew more concerned as she paused on the picture of Mrs. Wright. "Something wrong?"

"This is Mrs. Wright?" Mrs. Watson's finger glided across the face. "I think I have seen her. I was in a little bistro, and she was there talking to Mr. Jimenez. Isn't she a real estate agent?"

"Yes."

"Interesting. The way she was talking to Mr. Jimenez, it was as if they were clients of hers. Yes, she mentioned something, and she knew I was their attorney."

Detective Santiago reviewed the photo. "Are you sure? This photo is from the ER, she was pretty banged up"

"This is her. I saw her and overheard her conversation, which led me to talk to her. Interesting."

"Why would she talk to Mr. Jimenez? She doesn't have a good relationship with his wife and to my knowledge, never met or spoke to him." Detective Santiago quickly remembered that Juan pointed fingers at Jasmine as a person who would want to see Noemi go down for the death of her son.

"Thank you for your time. I have to go."

"No, thank you for stopping by." Detective Santiago waited for Mrs. Watson to leave before scooping the water bottle up to get her prints. He wanted to match her prints to the pocketknife.

Chapter 81

• • • •

DETECTIVE SANTIAGO stood next to Noemi's bed as she slept. He turned to Juan, ready to fire off questions. Juan looked worse for wear and a new patch of grey hair was forming at his hairline. "Mr. Jimenez, have you ever spoken to Mrs. Wright?"

Juan dragged his hand down his face, his jaw slack. "Never."

"You never saw her?"

"No, I have only heard about her from Noemi."

"She doesn't have your number?"

"No."

"She doesn't have your wife's number?"

"Not that I know of."

"Can you verify with your wife if Mrs. Wright has ever called her?"

Juan grabbed the detective's hand firmly, pulling him closer to him. "What's going on?"

"I'm just following up on something I heard. I will keep you posted." Detective Santiago patted Juan on the shoulder with his free hand.

• • • •

JASMINE SHOWED HER phone to Detective Santiago, scrolling through her contacts. "I have never had contact with her outside of school."

"You have had contact with her outside of school. The grocery store."

"What I mean is I have never called her. I don't have her number. I would go to the school and meet with the principal."

"You never contacted her husband?"

"I don't know him. I never spoke to him, nor have I ever seen him."

"Have you spoken to Mrs. Watson?"

Jasmine scratched her nose, placing her phone in her pocket. "Who is that?"

"Mrs. Watson says she saw you and you know who she is."

"I don't know any Watson lady. I don't know what you are talking about. Is this going somewhere?"

Detective Santiago shrugged his shoulders as he turned to leave. "Just following up on what I heard."

Chapter 82

MRS. WATSON HELD HER phone up for Noemi to view the screen. "Is this the mother of Chance?"

Noemi shook her head disgusted by the sight of Jasmine. "That's her, she's a realtor."

Mrs. Watson put the phone back in her purse. "Well, I was sitting across from her a day or so ago and she was talking to your husband. Basically, I was eavesdropping, but she said she was representing you. She said she was checking on you."

"Juan doesn't know her and she definitely did not talk to my Juan." Noemi muttered a few profanities then pointed at Juan's jacket, his phone was in the pocket. "You can check his phone. I can give you the code."

Mrs. Watson's retrieved the phone and punched in the code then turned the phone toward Noemi. Noemi skimmed through his phone log and no odd numbers showed up. "Every call is from people I know from his contacts. He never spoke with her."

"Interesting. She knew who I was and I told Detective Santiago that when I was looking at some of the evidence."

"She's up to something. I know her." Noemi reached for her cup of water. She swallowed a few sips, then started chewing on some ice. "They are saying I could be released in a few days."

Mrs. Watson smiled a genuine smile. "I'm meeting with the judge to have you released on bond. I don't think you are a danger to anyone and although they found incriminating evidence, it doesn't mean you have to sit in jail. You have nothing to do with that tragic accident. I will touch base with you and your husband after the hearing. Fingers crossed and you could be allowed to go home."

Noemi's hand trembled as she covered her face, tears fell as she tried to compose herself. "I have faith in you. God knows I do."

Chapter 83

• • • •

JASMINE FELT HER STOMACH churn, her mouth twisting before she violently vomited every last bite of dinner. She lurched forward to grab her phone, but vomit spilled down her blouse and onto her leggings. Through the chaos, she could hear Detective Santiago shouting for her on the other end of the line. Jasmine wiped spit from her chin with her sleeve. "The judge did what?"

Detective Santiago cleared his throat. "They are releasing Mrs. Jimenez on bond, she's still the main suspect."

Jasmine could feel chunks of lasagna around her lower gums. She got up, grabbed her water and gargled before spitting everything in the kitchen sink. "Thank you for letting me know." Jasmine peered down at the floor then at her clothes. She had to get cleaned up. She needed to prepare for Noemi's release.

• • • •

MRS. WATSON REPLAYED the footage from one of the neighbors' door camera. She turned to Juan with a smile on her face. "How did you get this?"

Juan crossed his arms over his chest. "I talked to my former neighbor and inquired about what their camera picked up that night Noemi was found in the pool. Really, after talking to Detective Santiago, I told him that he needed to look at Jasmine. Then I remembered that my neighbors motion detectors turn on with movement at the front of our old house so their camera had to start recording."

"So this footage is from that night and the camera caught a woman coming up to your house. I can't tell that it's Mrs. Wright, but let's get this to Detective Santiago."

Chapter 84

• • • •

JASMINE SAT WITH DETECTIVE Santiago, her mind racing and her nerves shot to pieces. "So there's nothing to be done? They are just going to let her go home and live her life when she is the main suspect? This is ludicrous."

Detective Santiago tapped the pen on the table. "I know this is hard for you to understand, but her lawyer put up a good argument. She's still a person of interest as she had a motive. We are still questioning people and gathering evidence for the state attorneys to use."

Jasmine gathered her belongings as she stood up. "Thanks for your help. I have no argument with you. It's the whole situation you see."

Detective Santiago glanced at his notes. "You ever been to Mrs. Jimenez's house...the one she moved from?"

"No." Jasmine's lips made a thin line.

"You never went to her house?"

"No."

"Not even with Mr. McGregor?"

Jasmine's eye twitched, and her gaze dropped to looking at the table. Her cheeks felt warm and her hands started to sweat. She didn't know where the detective was going with his line of questioning, but he knew something. "Yes, I assisted Mr. McGregor, but I did not know it was her house. I was just there to help with a showing."

Detective Santiago clicked his tongue on the roof of his mouth. Now this was a twist he wasn't expecting. "So you have been to her home? After you learned it was her house, did you ever go back?"

"No."

Detective Santiago replayed the recording from the neighbors' house. Jasmine watched. "This was the night she was found in the pool. That's you walking up to the house and entering it."

Jasmine quickly gathered her thoughts as she reached in her purse for her phone. "I really have to get back to my husband."

"You want to answer my question?"

"Not without my attorney present. I'm the victim here. You can't prove that's me." Jasmine's heart started pounding. She walked around the detective's desk and quickly left.

Jasmine sprinted to her car, nearly stumbling over her own feet as she desparately tried to distance herself from the police. Once inside, she drove home, determined to piece together what had happened the night Noemi was found in the pool. Reflecting on her responses during the conversation with the detective, she felt a wave of regret wash over her for how she had ended it. She definitely looked guilty.

• • • •

MRS. WATSON GLARED at Detective Santiago, she went from impressed with his summary of his interaction with Mrs. Wright to offended by his tactics. "Why are you insinuating that my client would want to hurt herself?"

Detective Santiago's lack of empathy was palatable. "Mr. Jimenez said that his wife mentioned wanting everything to end. He said she said that to you."

"She meant the situation...all of this." Mrs. Watson took in a steady breath, she needed to calm down.

"Do you recognize this?" He flung the evidence bag with the pocketknife in it across the table. The bag slid to the middle of the table.

Mrs. Watson leaned forward, looking at the pocketknife. "No sir."

"This was the pocketknife used to slash open Mrs. Jimenez's leg. We had it dusted for prints and the prints for Mrs. Jimenez and you came up. Now I'm wondering..."

Mrs. Watson's eyes opened wide. "I have never seen this and I did not give this to my client."

"Your prints are on it. Did you also give her the scalpel that she waved at our officer leading to her getting shot?"

"That's absurd. Why would I do that?"

Detective Santiago smiled. "Maybe you were trying to help your client. We will be bringing this to the judge's attention and block Mrs. Jimenez's release."

Detective Santiago grabbed the evidence bag as he left the interrogation room. This case was getting more and more convoluted. He didn't know who to go after but it was starting to look like everyone involved had some explaining to do.

Chapter 85

BRENT SHIFTED HIS WEIGHT from one foot to the other as he listened to Jasmine's explicative filled rant. There was so much going on, and she sounded frazzled. He went from room to room, making sure everything was just right. He headed downstairs putting his hand over the receiver of his phone. "Are you sure about this? Do you really want people coming through the house? Noemi will be home and needs time to get back to normal?"

Juan reassured Brent over his decision. "No time like the present, right?"

"Maybe we should get you all looking at houses first and then we can do a contingency that you have to close on a house before this one sells." Brent smiled briefly. "Let me give you a few minutes." He went outside to go sit in his car and continue his conversation with Jasmine. "Jasmine, sorry about that. I'm here with Juan. His wife is going to be home soon, and he wants to put the house on the market."

Jasmine paused to control her rage. "That's going to be one cold day in hell."

Brent placed his phone on speaker so he could get his tablet set up. "Jasmine, calm down. She's still the person of interest."

"They are still looking for the truck. That's part of the reason she's being released. They want to track down the truck. Last time I checked, they know the make and model."

Brent grabbed his water then remembered his wife's run in with the stranger who was inquiring about her truck. "Son of a..."

"What?"

Brent watched Juan come out the front door. "Listen, I will call you back." Brent quickly got out of the car and made his way up to Juan. "What did you think?"

Juan looked back at the door then back to Brent. "You are right. Let's get Noemi home then we can formulate a plan."

Brent smiled broadly, he clasped Juan's hand. "When is she coming home?"

"End of the week."

"Great, do you mind if I stop by on the weekend to touch base?"

"Sure, I really need to get us secure financially. We have enough lawsuits, and the insurance company only covers so much then it's our responsibility."

Brent gave Juan a pat on the shoulder. He needed to get back home and discuss the visitor with Ingrid. The more he considered it, the more certain he became that it was Detective Santiago.

Chapter 86

• • • •

ZOYA AND AALIA WALKED around the playground next to Lake Whetstone. They used to come here all the time but now they were there because Aalia wanted to see the scene of the accident. Weeks had passed and you could still see the tire marks on the road and the deep tracks made coming down the hill. Aalia walked along the sidewalk up to the path the car took into the water. She looked back up the hill. She walked halfway up the hill, watching the cars whiz past. She stepped over one set of tracks in the now hard ground. She saw the school emblem a few feet from her. She took a few steps and bent over. "Mom, a magnet." She grabbed the magnet and came running down the hill.

Zoya looked at the muddy magnet.

Aalia pointed back up the hill. "It was by the tire tracks. Did Mrs. Wright have one of these on her car? You said the truck had one."

Zoya held the magnet with two fingers, trying to not get her whole hand dirty. "I thought I saw the magnet on the truck in the recording. We should give this to the detective. You want me to ask Jasmine if it's hers?"

Aalia pointed at her mother's phone anxiously.

Zoya pulled up Jasmine's number and the phone only rang once. "Hi, that was quick."

Jasmine didn't even say hi back. "You know they are going to release her this week?"

"Wow, really?"

"Yeah. I'm livid. What's up? How are you?"

"I'm good. You know those school magnets you put on the car? Did you have one on your car?"

Jasmine laughed. "No, you couldn't pay me to put those on my car. I find them to be tacky."

Zoya looked at Aalia with some trepidation, but that soon became clouded by suspicion. If the magnet wasn't Jasmine's, it had to belong to the truck that ran them off the road. "Well, I just wanted to check in on you. We should get together this weekend, sounds like you need to vent some frustration."

"Sounds good to me. I will text you. You know they are going to sell their house."

"They are? They just got that house."

"Bleeding money. I will see that woman rot in hell. She can go home but she won't be there long."

Zoya looked at Aalia who was already halfway to the parking lot. Zoya placed the magnet in her bag.

Chapter 87

• • • •

AALIA WALKED AROUND the blacktop perimeter, watching other students clustered in groups talking. She could see the cars already lining up to pick everyone up. She rolled her eyes, knowing they still had another class, therefore an hour before dismissal. These parents really got to school early to sit. Aalia quickly ran into the gym teacher. "May I go to the bathroom?"

"Sure, then go directly to class. I'm sending your class back in a couple minutes."

Aalia knew gym was nearly over; she just needed an excuse to break away. Taking the long way around, she made sure to walk past the cars in the carpool line. Spotting her mother's car, she quickly headed over to the passenger side. "Early as usual."

Zoya smiled then feigned innocence. "You know I'm always right in front of the building."

"Did you talk to the detective?"

"Yes. Interesting conversation."

Aalia watched more parents arriving, her eyes grew wide as she saw Brent's dad pull up. "Mom, the truck is back. You should take a walk with Marlene and scope it out. Don't forget about the magnet."

Zoya watched her daughter run into the building. She craned her neck and took a good look at Brent in his truck. Her gaze was broken by the appearance of Marlene. Zoya got out of her car and stood with Marlene. "Brent has his truck back."

Marlene put her hand over her eyes, blocking the glare of the sun. "Let's take a walk."

Zoya and Marlene slowed their pace as they went around the circle to the bench. They had front row seats to look the truck over. Brent waved at them and they happily waved back. He was on the phone. Zoya covered a yawn. "There's no damage. It's just dirty."

"Yes, it's dirty but look at that clean spot. Looks like a school magnet could've been there."

Zoya looked at the perfectly clean circle. "Let's go talk to him and see how he's doing."

Marlene threw her hand in the air, gesturing dramatically at him. "He's on the phone."

Zoya turned so she was parallel to Brent. She seemed to be at the height she was when the truck sped past them. She tried to place herself back at that night. She was on the passenger side, the truck was behind them, then switched lanes and sped past them. "The magnet was on the driver's side."

Marlene got up and walked with confidence around the truck, coming to a stop in front of Brent's door. She watched at Brent lowered his window and that's when she realized she was straining to look up at him. He was a good foot above her head looking down at her. "What's up?"

Brent smiled down at her. "Nothing much. How are you?"

Marlene looked at him then at his super-sized tires. The step to climb into the truck was above her knee, matter of fact it was two steps. "How do you get into this thing?"

"I'm used to it. It's lifted too. I like driving and looking down on everyone." He waved off his comment as he laughed.

"How's Brent?"

"He's doing great. Just got to take it one day at a time." Brent picked up his ringing phone, shook it at Marlene, then rolled his window up. Marlene proceeded to walk past the truck, seeing the school magnet high up on the bed of the truck. She walked back over to Zoya. "I think you are on to something. But there's no damage."

Zoya grabbed her phone and took a couple pictures. "You still have the picture from the funeral? Remember there was a huge truck there. Did Brent come in that?"

"I don't think my picture caught if there was any damage but I do have it. We should talk to the detective again."

Chapter 88

• • • •

DETECTIVE SANTIAGO compared the two images as best as he could. The trucks were two different makes but very similar. He knew the make of the truck that belonged to the pieces found in the Jimenez's garage. There were several local residents with that truck in their possession but he couldn't dismiss that the truck owner was not from this area, county or even the state. Detective Santiago needed a good reason to look at the McGregor's trucks. He would have to do some more foot work because no judge was going to give him a warrant to gain access to look at their vehicles.

Detective Santiago parked in the teachers' lot, where he had a clear view of the parents lining up to pick up their children. As cars pulled up and idled, he noticed a distinct lack of trucks, with plenty of crossovers, a few jeeps, and numerous hybrid cars instead. Soon, his gaze landed on Brent and his truck, which stood out-without a single scratch or dent in sight. Detective Santiago had to do some more digging.

• • • •

JASMINE SAT IN HER car, biting her nails, as she patiently waited for Noemi to return home. She had to lay eyes on her. After an hour of sitting with no activity, she started her car. Her arms started to tingle and her back ached as she sat there. She remembered that Detective Santiago presented her with footage of her approaching Noemi's house. Maybe her being here was not a good idea. She quickly looked around her surroundings and drove off. The last thing she needed was another security camera catching her where she did not need to be. Jasmine rounded the corner and parked in front of Brent's house. She watched the garage door open letting Brent come out and walk down the driveway. She rolled her window down but decided to get out of the car. "Sorry to just show up. I was in the neighborhood."

Brent laughed as he crossed his arms across his chest. "Hopefully, you weren't by the Jimenez house?"

Jasmine blushed, a chuckle escaped her mouth. "Who, me?"

"Good, cause they aren't in town anyway." Brent smirked.

Jasmine's eyes squinted as she needed to get more information. "Where are they?"

"They went out of town for a few days. They can't go far, but Juan thought it would be a good idea for them to be anywhere but here for a few days."

"Can't face the music, huh?"

Brent looked at his watch, noting the time. He was already going to be late. "I have an errand to run. I will talk to you later." Brent waved Jasmine off so he could meet up with his brother-in-law, Jake. He got in the car and drove off. After making a quick pit stop, he eventually made it to Jake's shop. He pulled the car right into the open bay.

Jake wiped his hands on a towel. "How many cars are you going to get?"

Brent got out of the car, quickly giving Jake a firm handshake. "Can you lift this bad boy up? I swear something got up in the undercarriage."

Jake gave the car a good once over. "What did you do now? Not another deer hit? That last cleanup was the worst. I couldn't handle the smell."

"I hit a bad pothole and the car isn't driving right." Brent tossed the keys to Jake so he could position the car over the lift. As soon as the car was hoisted up Brent went under the car while Jake went to talk to a customer. Brent grabbed at a few cables and looked at the tires. He saw Brent Jr. park his truck in the parking lot, his ride had arrived. He finished fiddling with the car then grabbed a towel to wipe his hands as he walked over to Jake. "Take a look and check the suspension for me. Can you do me a favor? When you are done, call me and I will update you. I need you to put her on your flat bed and drop her off." He gave Jake another firm handshake, then headed to his truck. Brent Jr. slid over to the passenger side as Brent Sr. opened the driver's side door. "Thanks for coming for your old man."

Brent Jr. looked at the car then waved to his uncle. "You really go above and beyond for your clients."

Brent Sr. laughed. The ride home was going to be a silent one. He had a whole weekend with nothing to do. Surely he and his son could stir up some fun.

Chapter 89

• • • •

BRENT OPENED THE GARAGE as Jake reversed the car off the flatbed truck. Brent smiled as Jake slid the car right into its spot. "That's what I am talking about! Did you find any issues?"

Jake hopped out of the car, closed the door, then tossed the keys at Brent. "No big issues. I really didn't have to do much, she's not that old. I think I found what you were experiencing on the right tire, tightened up the suspension and she should be good to go."

Brent kicked the tire jokingly. "What do I owe you?"

"On the house, family discount." Jake got back to his truck and drove off.

Brent closed the garage door, then walked down the driveway and down the road to leave the neighborhood. Brent was fully out of breath by the time he made it to the main road. That last hill got him winded, but he enjoyed the scenic route. He needed to get back to his daily runs, but he had been so busy the past few weeks. He was determined to run to Lake Whetstone and back in under two hours.

• • • •

JASMINE POUNDED HER fists on her dashboard as she drove to her next listing. She was already running late but would still get there before her clients. She parked her car then hustled to the house. She punched in the code to get the key from the lockbox. She rang the bell to make sure the owners had left then unlocked the door.

She stood in the doorway, absorbing the atmosphere of the house before switching on more lights and inspecting each room. Spotting a pair of shoes, she quickly grabbed them and placed them next to the couch. As she looked up, her gaze landed on the pictures resting on the ledge beside the fireplace. She walked over to get a look at the family. A couple dogs, husband, and Mrs. Watson. Of all the houses, the attorney's house. Her fingers glided around the gold frame as a chilling smirk framed her lips. She quickly walked through the house, making her way to the upstairs bedroom. She turned on the lights, surveyed the room, then grabbed her gloves. She went through a few drawers then continued her walk through. She made her way back downstairs, grabbing a few objects and arranged them just so. The doorbell rang, startling her, making her remember what she was actually here to do. She quickly ran to the door allowing her clients in.

She listened to their apologies for being late but she didn't hear a word. She was preoccupied. The showing went rather well and the clients were very receptive to the house. Each pass through a room gave her more access than she needed and she was appreciative of their receptiveness. Jasmine escorted her clients to their car, ensuring she locked the house securely behind her and left it just as she had found it.

Chapter 90

••••

JASMINE STOOD OUTSIDE the Jimenez home with Brent. Her nose crinkled as she glanced around cautiously, clutching her purse tightly under her arm. She knew she shouldn't be here, yet here she was. Brent scampered up the stairs with the lockbox in hand. He set it by the step before unlocking the door.

Jasmine followed Brent inside, glad to be inside but concerned about her presence being known. "So, they are selling?"

Brent shrugged his shoulders. "Not sure yet, but I'm preparing. Juan is going to think about it. I'm here to make sure everything is all right while they are out of town."

"When are they returning?"

"I think tonight or tomorrow."

Jasmine rubbed her eye. "May I take a look around, just in case I have clients who you can show the house too?"

Brent waved Jasmine off. "Sure, I need a few minutes and we can go."

Jasmine strolled through the house methodically as she pulled on a new pair of gloves. She found her way to the garage looking at every inch of the room. She walked around the car, reached for the door, finding it unlocked. She quickly popped the trunk open and emptied her purse full of goodies into it. She removed the panel that covered the spare tire. She removed the tire, rolling it across the garage and tucking it behind some boxes. Jasmine made sure to put the cover back then closed the trunk. After passing through the kitchen she found Brent wrapping up whatever it was he was up to. "You know the house I showed yesterday was the attorney's house? Noemi's attorney."

Brent smiled to himself. "Well, that's interesting. Mrs. Watson, right? Yes, I'm handling her purchase, remember? She found a house so we need to sell her property."

"I didn't know it was her house until I saw her photos. It was rather interesting now that you mention it. Nice house. I made sure to make my rounds. You never know what you'll find in a house."

"Yes, you come across some interesting things when listing a home."

"Yes, you dig up a lot of stuff. Some things make you question your very existence."

Chapter 91

NOEMI TOOK HER MEDICINE as she looked at her message from Mrs. Watson. How dare Jasmine make demands. Now she was requesting her movements to be monitored. She would have to go to court to get a contraption wrapped around her leg. She slammed the phone on the counter, adrenaline coursing through her veins. She grabbed her keys and rushed to her car. She was literally out of the area for a few days only to come to this. She needed air, she needed to breathe, she needed to wrap her bony fingers around Jasmine's neck.

Noemi drove around, but all good things must come to an end. She had begun to make her way back home, she had left her phone at home and knew Juan would be looking for her. With no way to reach him, she prepared herself for a stern talking too. She could hear him now, annoyance in his voice, maybe some disappointment because he didn't trust her to do basic things like driving alone. She came to the stop light, drumming her thumbs to the beat. She heard a car honk at her and realized that the light had turned green. She stepped on the gas but the car stalled. She saw the cars start to go around her. Her cheeks started to feel warm, she stepped on the gas again and the car started to move forward. She glared at the next car honking at her and going around her, this car made sure to slow its roll and give her the finger.

Noemi blinked hard, realizing the driver was Jasmine. Her car sputtered back to life as she accelerated to catch up to Jasmine. All sane thinking had left the building as she sped up. She stepped on her brakes as Jasmine suddenly stopped short. Jasmine definitely knew it was her behind her. Noemi continued to follow Jasmine closely, running into the back of her car after another brake check from Jasmine. Noemi watched Jasmine speed off. Not today, Noemi thought to herself but how was she going to explain the possible dent to Juan? Noemi pressed her foot down on the gas pedal, whizzing past Jasmine and getting into her lane. She watched Jasmine in her rearview mirror, she wanted to return the favor and slammed her foot on her brake pedal. The car didn't slow down, she pumped the brakes...nothing.

Noemi glanced back at Jasmine, who was switching lanes to overtake her. As she looked at Lake Whetstone to her right, Jasmine suddenly swerved into Noemi's lane. In a panic, Noemi turned the steering wheel sharply to the right, veering over the curb. The car sped down the embankment, her forehead slammed into the steering wheel, and the vehicle flipped before crashing into the lake.

Jasmine stood on the curb, watching Noemi's car sink into the water. She quickly got back in her car and drove off. Jasmine pulled up to her house, made sure to inspect her car for damage, finding a crack in her fender. She flung the door open and got distracted by Craig, who was busy rummaging through the fridge. "What are you looking for?"

Craig looked back at her, a cabbage and carrots now in his hands. "Dinner for two."

Jasmine giggled then she remembered she was supposed to be upset. "You would not believe who hit me. She was trying to run me off the road."

Craig lost in thought cocked his head to the side, hearing sirens. "Must've been a bad accident. You hear all that commotion?"

Jasmine listened intently, knowing all that fuss must be for Noemi. She grabbed her keys. "Coming?" Jasmine rushed out the house with Craig in tow, they drove right back to the lake or at least as close as they could. Cars were backed up being nosy and rubber necking. She pulled over onto the median next to another car and watched as people stared at the crew. There wasn't much movement going on, seemed as though the car was further in the lake and they needed to drag the car out. An ambulance was waiting. Jasmine leaned against her car as all traffic going past the lake was blocked.

Jasmine remembered how dark the water was when she was trapped in her car, how she could barely see Chance. Nobody coming out of the lake felt good to her. The longer Noemi was down there, the higher the chance she was dead. Dead like Chance. A grin spread across her face. Her face lit up as the minutes passed. "She deserves all of this."

Craig wrapped an arm around Jasmine's shoulders. "What are you talking about?"

"Her!" Jasmine pointed at the lake, now illuminated by bright lights brought in to help with the recovery of the car. "Noemi."

"How do you know it's her?"

"I told you she tried to run me off the road. She hit my car."

Craig now started to understand what Jasmine meant. He escorted her to the passenger side of the car. "We are going home."

LAST CHANCE

Chapter 92

• • • •

JASMINE WOKE UP TO a headache and the doorbell. She looked across the bed, seeing Craig's side vacant. She grabbed her robe and ran downstairs. She could hear Craig talking to someone, the voice very familiar. "Detective Santiago."

Craig walked over to Jasmine, his face sullen. "Noemi is dead. Detective Santiago just wanted to inform us."

Jasmine put her hand up to silence Craig. She needed to determine if Detective Santiago was just here to relay the message or looking for more information. "She's dead? How?"

Detective Santiago rubbed his hands together. "Last night her car ran off the road and into Lake Whetstone. She was trapped in her car and drowned. They couldn't reach her in time."

"What about our case, it dies with her?"

"I am so sorry. There is not much we can do. Your case is still open because we haven't fully determined that Noemi was the suspect."

Jasmine looked at Craig as he ushered Detective Santiago out. She gathered her robe about herself as she walked to the couch, she turned on the TV, then took a long sip of Craig's coffee. "Don't offer Detective Santiago any information. He doesn't need to know that she hit my car. Let them come to us if at all with anything. Right now, I want to celebrate the death of Noemi Jimenez, may she burn in hell."

• • • •

ZOYA SCRUNCHED UP HER face as she opened the gym bag that was sitting a couple of weeks in the Lost and Found closet. The smell wafting from the gym clothes was overpowering. She zipped the bag shut and walked to the main office to return the key. The office was empty, but she could hear Mr. Walker shouting. She froze by the desk, her hand clutching the key, hovering over a half-eaten sandwich. A shadow passed in front of the slightly open door, the man was too tall to be Mr. Walker.

Mr. Walker pleaded his innocence but refused to lower his voice. "What exactly are you insinuating?"

"Were you and Mrs. Jimenez in some type of relationship? Were you protecting her?"

"No! No!"

"Were you feeding her information about the investigation against her and Chance?"

"No!"

Detective Sanchez walked past the door to the window. "Were you helping her embezzle money from the school fund?"

Mr. Walker's breathing became shallow, he was not sure what was going on, but he needed help. "Do I need a lawyer?"

"I think you need to come down to the station and answer some questions. I much rather you come on your own accord. I don't want to escort you in cuffs in front of all these nice parents." Detective Sanchez pointed at the line of cars already sitting in carpool.

Zoya dropped the keys on the plate with the sandwich just as the door swung open. Her mouth agape as she watched Detective Sanchez escort Mr. Walker out of the office. She turned as the secretary was entering. She nodded at her, then followed Mr. Walker out the front door, she quickly ran to Marlene's car. She couldn't open the door fast enough. "Holy crap!"

Marlene stared at Zoya. "What's Detective Sanchez here for?"

Zoya waved her hands frantically, she was starting to sweat. "He was questioning Mr. Walker and implied that he and Noemi were in a relationship. He may have been giving her information about the allegations of misconduct with Chance. And he may have been helping her steal money from the school."

"What the f-"

Zoya punched the air several times. "You can't make this crap up!"

Chapter 93

• • • •

TWO WEEKS HAD PASSED and many of the students and parents were in attendance at Noemi's funeral. Marlene sat with Sophie and Aalia while Zoya was paying her respects. The chatter went to a hush as Mr. Walker made his way up to speak with Juan and pass on his condolences. Marlene peered at the images of Noemi in the slide show as Zoya made her way back to her seat. The service was nice and not one dry eye was to be seen.

Marlene fanned herself as she watched a guest make her way up to the casket. Her stilettos clicking with each step and her blonde curls spilling out from her dark veil. She stood over Noemi for a good while then leaned in. Marlene's right eye started to twitch. Who was this lady? The service continued on.

Zoya crinkled her nose, a familiar smell triggered her. She sniffed, then covered her nose. She looked around and nobody seemed to be smelling it. She leaned forward to get Marlene's attention. Marlene's expression was blank. Zoya nudged Aalia, lowering her head as she whispered. "Do you smell that?"

Aalia shook her head quickly. "Smells like poop."

Zoya started to gag as she heard other people reacting to the odor. One of the funeral directors quickly walked over to the casket, took a look, then quickly shut the top and locked it. He quickly gathered his staff and they started to escort the casket to the hearse.

Marlene quickly gathered her things and met Zoya and the girls at their car. "What was that smell?"

Zoya sunk into her car seat. "Maybe someone stepped in poop."

"Oh my goodness, it was strong. Meet you at the cemetery."

At the gravesight. Zoya and Marlene were towards the back of the crowd. They listened to the priest say his blessings and watched as people went to place flowers on the casket. Zoya felt her shoulder get pushed forward as a woman made her way through the onlookers. The veiled woman was very determined to get past people. She had some purple flowers at her side as she stumbled forward. She shoved one student to the side, took two steps, then fumbled her way to the casket. In her attempt to break her fall, she tossed the flowers, threw her arms out, her hands slammed into the casket. The casket shifted then she propped herself up and got her footing. The woman gave her best push and watched the casket fall to the ground with a thud. Everyone gasped.

In all the commotion nobody was paying attention to the veiled woman as she scampered through the cemetery. She had ditched the stilettos when she arrived. She jogged back to her car, pulling the veil from her head with one hand and starting her car with the other. She glanced at her rearview mirror watching Juan staring at his wife's casket being picked up. He looked disturbed. Good. She laughed hysterically as she drove off while her phone sprung to life. "Hello?"

"Where are you?" Craig asked.

"I had to visit an old friend. You would not believe the day I have had. I volunteered to take our neighbors dogs out for a walk. You would not believe how much crap those dogs make. No worries, I had a special trash bin to dump it in." Jasmine smiled as she reveled in making sure Noemi got one last gift from her. Jasmine pulled the blonde wig off her head, tossing it out the window. Since Noemi crashed Chance's funeral, returning the favor was the least Jasmine could do.

Chapter 94

MARLENE AND ZOYA STOOD shoulder to shoulder by the front office watching the harried scene before them. Mr. Walker was pointing at his desk as he had his arm placed behind his back by Detective Sanchez. He yelled final commands to his staff before being pushed toward the front door. The police cars lined up along the horseshoe while parents already sitting in the carpool line watched on in disbelief.

Mr. Walker attempted to shrink away, but it was nearly impossible. For someone who thrived on being the center of attention, he certainly wasn't enjoying the spotlight now.

Marlene looked back at Mr. Walker's office as Jasmine made her exit with several folders in her hand. Marlene nudged Zoya then walked up to Jasmine. "What the heck is going on? Why are you here?"

Jasmine gave the folders a quick tap. "These idiots thought they were going to get away with it. Just because Noemi's dead doesn't mean I don't get justice for my son."

"Why is Mr. Walker being arrested?" Zoya spat the question out.

Jasmine leaned into the ladies, a smirk on her face. "Let's just say, he and Noemi were complicit and definitely were skimming funds off the top of the fundraisers. He's a bastard! He didn't take any of my claims seriously. The money trail was proved to be going right back to, both of them." Jasmine clutched the folders to her chest. "I got to go. I have a listing to get ready to show. Talk to you two later."

Marlene and Zoya watched her leave, she made a pit stop by Brent's truck then walked to her car that was sitting in the teachers' parking lot. Marlene grabbed Zoya by the arm, dragging her over to Brent's truck. "Hey Brent, what the what?"

Brent looked down at the ladies, his elbow perched on the window. "Isn't this wild? Jasmine told me he was helping Noemi steal money. Crazy! He is always begging for funds and pandering to us parents and all this time he was stealing. Wow!"

"Jasmine was here with evidence?" Marlene's top lip quivered as a chill went down her spine.

"Nah, she was there for a meeting. I could've sworn she said the meeting was around noon." Brent showed his carpool number to the teacher walking around with the tablet. "You think she was here all that time?"

Marlene shook her head unaware of the answer. "I wonder what the meeting was about?"

Brent shrugged his shoulders. "I didn't ask, she just told me she had a meeting." Brent's phone went off as he waved at the ladies.

Marlene and Zoya walked back to their cars. They stood between the cones expressionless. "You think the girls heard any gossip?"

• • • •

JASMINE SAT ON CHANCE'S bed clutching the diploma he got. An honorary diploma. His GPA still short, no cap and gown, no walking across the stage. Just a diploma printed out by the school to save face. School was coming to a close. Chance's class was graduating in two weeks. Tears streamed down her cheeks as she looked at his name. She got up, taking the most complicated steps over to his desk, placing his diploma on the shelf.

She turned toward Craig, whose presence she felt looming in the doorway. "It's not fair! All of his friends are going to head off to college, get married, have kids. Not my Chance. His life cut down. Noemi is gone and I was able to witness Mr. Walker get arrested. Oh how low he must've felt being escorted out in handcuffs in front of all those parents. Who is he going to pander to now? Idiot!" Jasmine pointed at the diploma. "I'm going to make sure everyone who wronged my baby, goes down."

Craig grabbed Jasmine by the shoulders. "It's done. Noemi is dead. Anything that could have been resolved died with her. We still can't say she killed our son."

Jasmine wiped her nose with the back of her hand. "It was Noemi. It was the principal. They let our son down. I won't rest until I get justice for my baby."

Chapter 95

••••

BRENT SR. LOOKED AT the graduation invitations one last time before placing them in the mailbox. Graduation was two weeks away and there was still so much to do. Ingrid was busy planning the graduation party and the seniors were already home. Brent looked at his son as he played his video game. In a couple months they would be dropping him off at college. Brent smiled at the bright future that laid before his son.

Brent grabbed his phone, he needed to check in with Jasmine. This had to be a tough time for her, with all the graduation events coming up. The phone call went to voicemail. He decided not to leave a message this time. Brent looked back in the playroom then headed up the stairs. "I'm going to Lake Whetstone." He yelled to nobody in particular. By the time he made it to his truck he could hear Brent Jr. running up behind him. "You want to drive?"

Brent Jr. reversed the truck out of the driveway. His palms suddenly damp with sweat. "Dad, I'm worried about school. I still don't know what I want to study."

"Don't worry about that. You don't even have to pick a major until your third year." Brent Sr. play punched his son in the arm. They arrived at Lake Whetstone and parked. The sky got cloudy and dark. A few drops of rain quickly escalated to a downpour.

Brent Sr. put his chair to recline. "So, Mr. Walker still hasn't returned to the school?"

"Nope, I think he's on leave. The school never put out a memo on him, huh?"

"No. That's the weird part. They shouldn't be silent on this. They need to be transparent."

"Is it wrong that I don't feel bad?"

"Feel bad about what?"

Brent Jr. squirmed in his seat. "I spoke with that investigator for the school about Chance. At no point did I feel sorry for him."

"That investigation isn't done? I mean the main suspect is dead." Brent Sr. stared out at the lake. The rain started to ease up. "Ready for a walk?"

The walk around the lake took an hour. Father and son were in good spirits and had a healthy conversation about what the upcoming freshman year should be like. Brent Jr. feeling much more sure of himself after their talk released some stress with a stretch. "Dad, I just want to say thank you. You have always had my back. How do you keep it together with Mrs. Wright? I mean you are friends right?"

"I am able to compartmentalize things. You do too. You have had a tough year. That night was just a rough one."

Casino Night

Jasmine and Brent Sr. stood in the doorway to the gym, dressed to the nines and ready to participate in the school fundraiser. Casino Night was already off to a good start. Parents were participating in the silent auction, others were playing legit casino games and the house was definitely going to win. "Good job, Brent." Her eyes glided over the room taking in everyone and everything. She spied the bar and made her way over with pep in her step. She tapped Zoya on the shoulder. "How many drinks have you had?" A toothy grin spread across her face.

"This is my third glass of Chardonnay. Marlene over here brought her own bottle."

Marlene giggled. "Hey, don't say that out loud. She brought some rum punch." Marlene pointed at Zoya's embroidered bucket purse.

"You two are not playing. Can I have some of the rum punch?" Jasmine reached for a cup and winked at Zoya. "Fill her up!"

The trio hung out and were definitely acting the fool the whole time. They were having a great time. They made their way to the silent auction tables, then played a few hands of poker. Jasmine turned from the table as she heard a commotion. People were huddled by the entrance and appeared to be in a tizzy. She tapped Zoya and pointed at the door. "I wonder what that is all about?" Jasmine took a sip of her drink finishing it in one swift gulp. A warm burn spread through her chest and her face flushed. She was a few drinks in, and dinner hadn't even been served yet. As she surveyed the crowd, she noticed it parting to reveal Noemi Jimenez strolling through, flanked by a few other teachers who looked like part of a power squad.

Zoya, sensing the distress, put a hand over Jasmine's clenched fist. "Breathe!"

"I'm good!" Jasmine screeched. "Why is she here?"

Zoya waved at Mr. Walker who appeared to see Jasmine's reaction and was already heading in their direction. Mr. Walker stood in front of Jasmine, blocking her view of Noemi. "I didn't know she was coming. Technically, there are no children here, but I will request that she leaves."

Jasmine released her fist and got up to get to her table. The food was being sent out. "Brent or Zoya, can one of you get a bottle of red wine sent to our table?" Jasmine left in a huff and found a seat. She started eating bread and stabbing at her salad with her fork. The bottle of wine arrived, and she promptly poured her glass almost to the brim. She took a couple sips then got up to get some air. She walked the perimeter of the gym and strutted between a few tables until she could see Noemi. She watched her standing next to another teacher, tossing her head back in a fit of laughter. Jasmine felt the irritation burrowing more and more into her very soul. Her pace quickened and she pushed a parent to the side, pretended to trip, threw the glass full of red wine at Noemi's back and stumbled off as she heard Noemi gasp and the gaggle of women shriek.

Jasmine looked back long enough to see women trying to dab at the stain of wine covering Noemi's beige dress. Aww, too bad for her. Noemi quickly rushed out of the gym. Jasmine watched her leave, proud that she had removed the trash from the event. She quickly went to the bar to get a new wine glass and went to her seat as if nothing had happened. She was too smooth with it. She stabbed at her salad again, a broad smile spread across her face.

Ingrid ran around the table to observe the chaos and make sure none of her people were hurt. The last thing she needed was for her staff to be involved in an incident. Her eyes darted from Noemi to the women surrounding her trying to help. Soon, her gaze fell upon her husband, Brent, scoffing down some salad. That man was not phased at all. He was definitely observing the madness. Assured that there was nothing she needed to do, Ingrid gathered her staff and prepared to have the next course delivered to each table. "Start clearing the tables and you can begin serving the second course. Ingrid watched Noemi scamper towards the ladies room. She felt bad for her. Not that bad, though. There was too much going on for her to be too concerned.

Mr. Walker made his way over to Ingrid to share his gratitude. "Mrs. McGregor, this has been a success."

Ingrid smiled. "Oh, it was a pleasure to cater this event and it puts my business out there. This has been my largest catering job."

Mr. Walker looked around the room. "We can definitely use your services next year."

Ingrid clapped her hands together with glee and appreciation. She tilted her head spying Brent fawning over Jasmine. He spent way too much time with her. Her smile quickly turned to a smirk. "If you will excuse me, I need to talk to Brent." Ingrid went out of the gym and stood by the bathroom. She actually needed air so she went outside and walked over to her catering truck. She leaned on the bumper as she pulled out her phone. She saw Mrs. Jimenez sitting in her car, she looked extremely upset. Ingrid minded her business as her son answered her call. "Hey, you can do me a favor? I need you to come here and help me pack up some stuff. Your father is over here having too much of a good time hanging out with Jasmine and friends."

Ingrid ended the call and walked over to Mrs. Jimenez's car, and she tapped on the window. "Are you all right?"

Mrs. Jimenez lowered her window, shaking her head apologetically. "I am fine. I am just going to get myself together. I can't believe what happened to me. It's just embarrassing. Don't worry about me. The night is still young."

Ingrid tapped the roof of the car then went back inside. As soon as Brent Jr. reached she had him pack up some of the bigger items into her catering truck. Brent Jr. completed his task and asked to stay just in case his mother needed more help. Brent Jr. waved at his dad, then turned back to his mom. She gave him the keys and waved him off. Brent Jr. walked across the parking lot and sat in the truck. He watched videos on his phone while he waited. The night finally seemed to be wrapping up. He watched his mom and dad have some words, his mother storming back in the gym. Then, Mrs. Wright came stumbling out, grabbing on his father's arm to balance herself. They were both drunk. Brent Jr. watched Chance pull up to the curb to retrieve his mom. She was a mess. She fell against the door then Brent Sr. opened the door for her.

Brent Jr. shook his head, laughing at the whole scene. The Wrights pulled out of the parking lot and another car left behind them. Brent Jr. called his mom. "Is Dad all right?"

Ingrid huffed in the phone. "You go home."

Brent Jr. didn't need to be told twice. He started the truck and left. He followed behind Mrs. Jimenez who was driving erratically but also very fast. He soon realized that she was following Chance and his mother. The road was empty but for a few cars. He followed Mrs. Jimenez who switched lanes and sped up just so she could overtake the Wright's. Brent Jr. followed suit, turned on his high beams and followed the car closely. They came up on the lake fast. Brent Jr. came up on their bumper and quickly changed lanes but overcorrected himself and turned the steering wheel back towards the car. His truck slammed into Chance's driver's side, the car slid up and over the curb and went over the embankment. Brent Jr. swerved back into his lane and kept driving. He watched the headlights fade down the hill but he kept driving until he got home and pulled into the garage. He got out of the truck and stood there waiting.

A few minutes, later his parents arrived. He ran to his dad's side of the truck. "Dad!"

Brent Sr., seeing the distress in his son's face rushed out of the passenger side. He followed him to his truck to look at the damage. "What happened?"

"I hit the Wright's car. Lake Whetstone!" Bent Jr. stammered. "I think I did it on purpose. I knew it was Chance in the car. I...I!"

Brent Sr. paused his son from continuing. "We need to pick up the van. You will drive the van back from the school. Don't say anything. Don't even mention this. I will have your uncle fix my truck up like new."

Brent Jr. looked up at his dad then to his mother who was now standing in the garage. "Two birds with one stone, right, Mom?"

Ingrid stood there confused. "What the F-?"

LAST CHANCE

Chapter 96

• • • •

JASMINE SUFFERED THROUGH the silence. The graduation parties were happening all around her, yards littered with congratulatory signs, she noticed the invitations to said parties never made their way to her. They of course, felt sorry for her because her son wasn't here to partake in any of the festivities. She did get one invite from the school so she could cross the stage for her son. The same stage that was being held just out of reach by the same school. At least Mr. Walker wouldn't be there. The assistant principal would host the commencement. Such a shame for Mr. Walker. Now he was shackled down by legal woes. Too bad he was found to be assisting Mrs. Jimenez in supplementing their lifestyles by stealing money from the school. Too bad Mr. Walker was found complicit in ignoring Chance's pleas for help. Too bad the Archdiocese offered up a hefty settlement.

Jasmine along with Craig held onto each other as they heard Chance's name, they rose from their seats to cross the stage that was so relentlessly taken from their son. It was his moment but here were his parents to cross for him. An honorary diploma because he never completed high school. He didn't get to submit all his work, he was removed from the basketball team, he was dead and buried...forever 17 years old. Jasmine's eyes glazed over as she passed the teachers. Too bad Mrs. Jimenez wasn't here to see this...wait, she didn't deserve to be here. She deserved to be dead. She deserved to be disgraced. She deserved to be looked at differently. Now everyone knew she was a thief and was hooking up with the principal. Well, at least that is how Jasmine left the evidence...may people draw the conclusions themselves. Too bad Mr. Jimenez now had to question his wife's fidelity. Too bad he lost their home.

Jasmine and Craig didn't stay to watch the rest of the ceremony, they ventured outside to sit on the new bench in honor of their son. Her fingers traced the dedication slowly as the warm breeze brushed through her bangs and over her ears. The air grew still, with not one animal sound breaking the silence, until the gym doors opened, releasing the graduates. Jasmine locked eyes with Ingrid who returned her gaze with a glare. Maybe the sunlight was in her eyes. Brent Sr. patted Ingrid's shoulders then waved as he made his way over to them. Jasmine looked at Brent Jr. getting up to give him a firm handshake. "Congratulations, young man!" All these years, and she didn't really know Brent Jr. not even in passing. "I'm sorry Chance couldn't be here."

Brent Jr. stared defiantly into Jasmine's eyes. "I'm not!"

Brent Sr. nudged Brent Jr. directing him to go by his mother. "He's tired. It's been a long day. It was good to see you all here for Chance."

"I didn't want to come but Craig thought it was a nice gesture." Jasmine patted the diploma case. "The real one is at home."

Brent Sr. escorted Jasmine and Craig to their car. He watched them drive off before heading over to his truck, Brent Jr. was already in the driver's seat. They drove off, following the Wrights. Ingrid patted the diploma sitting on her lap. She was so proud of her son. He was going to accomplish so much. As they drove next to the Wrights, they started to pass Lake Whetstone. She could see Jasmine having a good cry and Craig just trying to get home. It had to be so difficult for them to be at the graduation. Ingrid grabbed the steering wheel tugging it to the right. The truck swerved into the right lane. Craig looked up at them. Ingrid waved and mouthed a quick sorry then pointed to Brent Jr. "New driver!"

"Mom!"

"What, déjà vu!" Ingrid laughed hysterically all the way home.

Also by Sasha Welter

Revenge
Wicked Sisters
Last Chance

Milton Keynes UK
Ingram Content Group UK Ltd.
UKHW020020271124
451585UK00013B/1375